Minyan

Ten Interwoven Stories

Minyan

Ten Interwoven Stories

by

John J. Clayton

PARAGON HOUSE
Saint Paul

First Edition 2016

Published in the United States by
Paragon House
St. Paul, Minnesota

www.ParagonHouse.com

Library of Congress Cataloging-in-Publication Data

Names: Clayton, John Jacob, author.
Title: Ten interwoven stories / by John J. Clayton.
Description: First edition. | St. Paul, MN : Paragon House, [2016]
Identifiers: LCCN 2015047801 | ISBN 9781557789204 (softcover :
acid-free paper)
Classification: LCC PS3553.L388 A6 2016 | DDC 813/.54--dc23 LC
record available at http://lccn.loc.gov/2015047801

Manufactured in the United States of America

10 9 8 7 6 5 4 3 2 1

The paper used in this publication meets the minimum require-
ments of American National Standard for Information Sciences—
Permanence of Paper for Printed Library Materials, ANSIZ39.48-1984.

For Sharon, my first, best reader.
And, as always, for my son Josh.

Contents

Minyan 1

Children of Peace. 27

O'Malley Recites the Kaddish. 53

The Grandparent Option 83

A Question of Heart 111

The Gift 137

Cleaning Up a Mess 161

Whispers from a Distant Room. 191

The Embezzler and the Rabbi. 213

Forgiveness 243

Minyan

TUESDAY MORNING, a cold, clear January day. Here's Sam Schulman, mid-fifties, hearty in the sunny cold, his breath a mist in front of his mouth, blue velvet prayer bag in hand. An old gray stone building on Beacon Street in Brookline Massachusetts: B'nai Shalom. Sand blasters already at work: the swastika has been expunged. Faintly, *Stop Israeli Apartheid* comes through as pale erasure of the spray paint. Sam winces. The large, professional sign for the synagogue is gone. A new sign, temporary — marker on paper laminated onto poster board — replaces the stolen sign.

He shakes his head and shakes his head. There's never been a society more welcoming to Jews than America. But always there are sick haters. A redundancy: are there any *non*-sick haters? Isn't hatred itself, hatred against a whole people, evidence of sickness? Of self hatred, humiliation, directed away from the self?

Who did it? Skinheads? He supposes. Must be.

His key, stiff in the lock of the main door to the synagogue, finally turns. He makes a mental note: *Ask Stephanie in the office to have the lock oiled.* He touches fingers to lips, then to the mezuzah on the door jamb.

Inside almost as cold as outside — the synagogue thermostats kept low to save heat. Walking down the corridor past the library, past the large sanctuary, with the same key he opens the small sanctuary, a little room filled with morning light from clerestory windows above. He's never stopped feeling a leap in his heart when he enters the light inside.

And soon, he assures himself, he'll be warm. He adjusts the thermostat.

He's alone. Covering himself with his tallit, he wraps himself in the metaphorical wings of God and whispers a blessing. Now, still cold, he binds himself with his tefillin — wraps the straps of one leather box around his arm and lays the other box on his forehead. The leather is cool against forehead and arm. Both boxes contain, in tiny script, passages from Torah on the unity of God and the commandment to wear tefillin, and he tries, each day, at home or in synagogue, to imagine the straps binding him to God in *actions* (his arm) and in *thought* (his head). Usually, at home, it feels a mechanical ritual, feels more real at synagogue.

Almost every Tuesday is like this: for five, even ten minutes no one except Sam present in the minyan. Even when the others come, it's unusual for them to add up to ten adult Jews — a complete minyan — especially in winter, when the snow birds fly south. Gershom Samuels, for instance, always at minyan when he's in town — now off with his wife to visit his grandchildren. Before anyone else is in the sanctuary, Sam stands facing the ark and begins to chant. Come on, acknowledge it, he likes being a prayer leader with no one to lead: likes the solitude, while of course he also hopes there'll be a quorum of ten or more adult Jews, so communal prayers can be prayed.

He especially hopes for that today. It's his son's *yahr-zeit*, the second anniversary of the day Bennie died.

Two years ago, when his older son, then a third-year student at Yale, fought testicular cancer and lost (in denial, Bennie let it go and let it go) Sam organized this minyan at his synagogue so he, and others, could say Mourners Kaddish when in mourning or observing a *yahrzeit*. The Tuesday morning minyan has been, yes, yes, at times a weight—always to be there at 7:30 in the morning, no matter how tired, even sick, he's been. But it's also kept him whole.

Two years of grief. Hard to believe it's been so long. And it doesn't go away, you can hardly say it even diminishes the pain, the terrible loss—his beloved older son—almost every day it hits him freshly, not as *memory*—hits him as if he'd just now been informed. And then he groans—inwardly if he's around other people, outwardly if he's alone. Of course the pain is particularly intense today—the day has come round again.

It's warmer now. Facing the ark, not the congregation, as prayer leader he's almost finished chanting the Preliminary Service. Kate Schiff has come in. He tries to focus, not to look at her as intensely as he wants. His heart has always opened to Kate, though he hardly knows her—and though he's much too old for her. He knows her age from a Shabbat when she went up onto the bima one Saturday for a birthday blessing. She's thirty-six; he's fifty-five. Nineteen years. Embarrassing. He won't even try. Of course not. But with imagined fingers he strokes her long, light brown hair and touches her cheek.

And then Peter Weintraub enters—wild, curly, graying hair. Strange bird in glasses that give him an owlish look, flying as if from some other universe. Now Alex Koenigsberg, Professor of History at Tufts, comes in out of the cold, rubbing his hands together ferociously, as if the friction could start a fire. Sam looks over his shoulder, nods, smiles, returns to chanting psalms. Now the Singers, making seven, the usual first seven. Now a young man he doesn't know—he's seen him at services. The lovely Hebrew School teacher with her baby. He knows now there'll likely be a full minyan, for the tenth, Nick Shorr, the synagogue Executive Director, will stop by on his way to his office.

And Nick does. Earlier than usual they've made a complete minyan.

Sam's living son, Gabriel, is not among them. Each time the door opens, he turns his head, hoping. Last night he left a message on Gabe's phone to remind him that today is his brother's *yahrzeit*. "The day your brother left us," he said. But Sam doesn't really expect Gabe to come.

By the time they are to say the Mourners Kaddish,

there are fourteen in the little sanctuary. He's grateful. Now out of the corner of his eye Sam sees someone slip into the sanctuary. He turns from the ark for a moment— sees, yes, Shira, once his wife, Bennie's mother, Gabriel's mother, take up a prayer book and stand at the back. Just a glance does it. Her short, curly black hair, colored so subtly. Her lovely, long neck. The way she holds her head at a slight angle that he can read as self consciousness. Shira. This is a shock, but he finishes the *Aleinu* and announces the first recitation of Mourners' Kaddish.

*Yit gaddal v' yitkadash shmey rabboh . . .*The prayer, in Aramaic, doesn't speak of death or of the beloved dead; it's an affirmation of God, of God's holiness and glory. One or another Kaddish transitions between parts of a service. Mourner's Kaddish is simply one more Kaddish, this one recited, not chanted, by mourners. Yet it shakes Sam.

As services end and those in the minyan fold and put away prayer gear, Sam feels a touch on his arm. He looks around. It's Kate. Her hand. She says quietly, "May you be comforted."

"Thank you." He avoids her eyes. He keeps feeling the place on his arm she touched.

After services he wants to talk to Shira, but Tom Russell buttonholes him. As Chair of the Executive Committee, Sam has an obligation to listen.

"Sam? Have the police found the people who stole our

sign and did the spray painting? Are they even trying?"

"Nazis, I guess. Anti-Semites," Sam says, shrugs, sighs. "Police are asking questions. Excuse me, Tom."

Shira folds her tallit into her handbag. Most of the others know Shira or used to know her when she and Sam were together. They say words of comfort as they pass her on their way to work. Sam puts away tallit and tefillin, hurrying in order to speak to her.

After all, they're not enemies.

What happened when Bennie died? She'd been too sick with grief even to attend the funeral. He tried not to judge. Into the grave he dropped a shovelful of dirt for her. They grieved separately. No one was to blame. Bennie had never told them anything, not until his back began to hurt bad. And then hurt worse, past the ability for ordinary painkillers to do much. And by the time he had tests and more tests, the cancer had spread inoperably. To lungs and brain. He lived three months. While he slept in an induced coma, his heart gave up.

Why couldn't they comfort one another, he and Shira?

Those first months, when one of them wept, the other would leave the room. When they were in the same room, they didn't look at one another. When they spoke, it was about shopping, about schedule. They told each other it was essential to stay close to Gabe, then sixteen. They planned to take long walks with him, and sometimes they did so, but not knowing what to say, they often let him go his own way.

To Gabe they spoke gently. But not to each other. To each other they were polite and distant. Increasingly they spoke in curt, hostile sentences. The language of telegrams. Why? Twice, three times, this speech curdled into a small quarrel. One day, seven months after Bennie's death, Sam came home from work to find Shira gone. His wife of more than two decades. Her clothes gone. Her favorite wing-backed chair gone. Her computer, her printer. The molas she loved, the kilim, a couple of paintings. The rest she left. No negotiations, no explanation. Simply as if she were following Bennie in departing. Then, last January, Shira appeared at the unveiling. Somehow they found themselves able to talk again, but there was no talk about getting back together, no talk about Bennie. Negotiations over money, over financing of Gabe's education, that's all.

When Shira left, Gabe stayed at first with his father. Then he took the 'T' back and forth, apartment to apartment, both in Brookline, one week at his father's, the next at his mother's. He became more and more sardonic, aloof. Once, in an aside, he told his father, "I'm never getting married." Now he's a first-year at Boston University—in the same city but living with a roommate in a dorm. If he talks at all, except to answer questions, it's to speak cynically about Israel. Why Israel?—maybe just to get his father's goat, his mother's goat. "You loved Israel when you went there on the Birthright program. What happened?"

"I found out what's going on."

Sam hates ideological conflict. Especially with his son. Especially when he knows that the ideology is simplistic: *what's going on.* So *much* is going on. And especially when he knows that the ideology is just a cover. It's really about Bennie, it's really about us—his parents. Still, Sam makes a mental note to call Gabe today, to commiserate with him, to remember Bennie, to take and give comfort.

Glancing at Shira, glancing again as he lines up prayer books on a shelf of the glass-fronted bookcase of the small sanctuary, he finishes, nods to her. "It was good of you to come." She doesn't answer. At once he realizes he's all wrong—speaking as if he belonged here and she were a guest, as if he were the mourner and she there for him.

"I needed to say Kaddish too."

"Right, right. Of course." He taps his forehead, acknowledging his stupidity. "I'm glad." (Though, in fact when has she said the Mourner's Kaddish? Not ever, as far as he knows, not for Bennie, not for her parents, who died together in an auto accident.)

He watches her find her car key in her handbag, watches her stall. He asks: "Listen. So. You want to go for coffee?"

He says this to relieve her of the need to ask—because he knows she came mostly to speak to him. Of course. He knows that. There's a coffee place up a couple of blocks on Beacon Street. She drops the key back into her handbag and, not looking at him, accompanies him, walking fast this cold morning, as if they had to get somewhere in a hurry, though he hasn't got a class to teach till noon, and she opens the gallery at 10:00.

They stand in line for coffee, find a table by the window. He glances at her. Still a beautiful woman, he thinks. But her looks don't mean a damn to him. As if holding a talisman, he lets himself remember Kate Schiff. He uses her image to keep Shira at bay.

On Beacon Street a trolley heads downtown; at the corner by the synagogue it passes a trolley heading outbound.

"Two years," he says, as prompt for her to speak.

She nods, repeats his words. He feels foolish that after all the time—twenty-three years—they were together, that this is all they have to say; that all they have to mark time by now is Bennie's death. Why in God's name had they been together?

"I want you to know," she says, "that Avram and I are going to live together. He's going to move in at the end of the month. And what I mean is: we're going to *marry*."

"Good. Good. I hope you'll be happy."

"Sam? Avram needs me to have a Jewish divorce as well as a civil divorce. It costs. He'll pay."

"So—in front of a rabbinical court? A *bet din*? Of course you'll need me there."

"I will. If possible. The Bet Din is set for next Monday morning. Tentatively. You don't teach Mondays, right?" A long pause. "I hear they may try to talk us out of it."

"We're not children."

She puts her hand on his. In this act of deepest separation they are together — together for a few seconds. He says, "You want a really clean slate, don't you? You want to expunge the past."

"Of course I do. *Some* of the past. But that's not it. I believe in the future."

He winces at her cliché. He doesn't want her to think he's putting her down, but it's been a long time since they've seen each other, and he can't stop. "Listen. There must be something good about our past. Remember Martha's Vineyard? The kids were very little. Remember? We broke clay from the cliff at Gay Head and covered ourselves and let it dry? As if we were clay sculptures. Gabe refused to smear himself. He took pictures of his wild family. Remember?"

Shira doesn't respond. She smiles a weak smile.

"Then we dived into the ocean, we dived in and washed off the clay. Remember? We felt clean. We felt fresh."

She nods a weak nod; she's thinking of other things. It annoys him. He wonders: does she think he wants them to get back together? God knows, he does not. He's clear about that. With her gallery's second-rate art, with her rap music meant (he's sure) to tag her as cool and up to date. With her subscription to *Harpers Bazaar*. If he doesn't want her, then what *does* he want? Perhaps for them to mourn together. As if — and he knows this is stupid — as if until they mourn together, really together, Bennie won't rest easy. He sighs. "What time on Monday?"

The Bet Din of Boston meets upstairs in an century-old commercial building off the Common. Their footsteps echo on the old, musty staircase. Three gray-bearded men in fedoras sit at a table and listen to the request for a Jewish divorce. Though an observant Jew, though he leads services, he's not like these men in their beards and ear locks and black suits. One has a black gabardine coat belted between upper and nether body.

These Jews seem more foreign to him, a liberal, "worldly" Jew, than would Roman Catholic priests or Buddhist monks. But he respects them, even admires them.

It's not, for the old men, pro forma, this divorce. The men actually argue, or plead, with him and with Shira. They want to see if the marriage can still be saved. This seriousness moves Sam — moves both of them. They look at each other. He recognizes the trembling at the sides of her lips that means she's on the verge of crying — or giggling. An expression of nerves. Why giggling? It's the comedy of three men working to save a marriage long lost. To help her, he keeps his face a deadpan so she won't laugh. They feel — both of them, he's sure — like conspirators acting roles in a strange play.

It's only he, Samuel, the husband, *Samuel ben Yaakov* (son of Jacob), who finally has an active part to play. He is to write a *get* and hand it to his wife. Actually, one of the men of the court acts as scribe. Shira's only job is to accept the *get* from Sam's hand and hold it up high. This ritual gesture is surprisingly painful. The *get* is then ripped horizontally and vertically to prevent its being used again and is filed away by the *bet din*. Once the legal process is complete, the three rabbis are smiling, laughing, and shaking hands.

In a little more than an hour Shira and Sam are walking down the stairs together, oddly closer. They've been through something solemn. They still feel the sound of the rips. Shira's not at the edge of giggling now; she's at the edge of crying. She blows her nose into a tissue, says, "Avram's meeting me at a coffee shop on Charles. Will you come say hello?"

"I've got to get to school. I'm chairing an oral exam."

"Then what about stopping by early this evening for a drink? Avram wants to make sure you'll feel okay being members of the same synagogue. He wants there to be peace."

"Believe me, I feel peaceful toward Avram. I do. And toward you, Shira. But I'll stop by and toast the two of you."

Shira lives in a condo halfway between Beacon and Commonwealth. Even in the cold it's in easy walking distance of Boston University, where Sam teaches, where he's been teaching for two decades. His field is nineteenth century novel. He leaves his car in the B.U. garage. Walking to Shira's in the dark, he thinks what a hullabaloo his

Dickens or Eliot or James would've made over a visit by an ex-husband to an almost remarried wife. In our time it's not such a big deal. Anything that will help normalize Shira's life, his life, Gabe's life, is good. He's met Avram once, briefly, at a party at the synagogue. It's as if Shira wants him to look her new man over, even give his blessing. As if he, Sam, were . . . favored uncle. And he's anxious, frankly, to check out her choice.

It's a second and third floor duplex. Clean, bright, expensive, simple furniture. Paid for by Avram? Certainly with his help. Avram works as a lawyer in downtown Boston, and between the two incomes Sam guesses they do better than all right. A lot better than Sam. It's Shira who comes to the door, wearing tight jeans and a pale cream blouse he remembers from when they were together.

Avram comes from the kitchen, where he's probably been washing dishes — he's wearing a stained apron and a knitted white yarmulke. Left hand around Shira, with his right he pumps Sam's hand. Sam has an epiphany. *This* is who Avram is: *man in apron, man who wants to be connected. Good man in yarmulke. Kind, a kind man.* Shira has told him Avram is five years younger than Sam; he looks ten years younger. This makes Sam uneasy. A flashing thought: is Shira too old to have another child? Maybe not! She's forty-three. Maybe not.

Avram has put out cheese and crackers; there are three stemmed wine glasses and a bottle of prosecco in a ceramic cooler on the coffee table. Sam grunts positive comments about the apartment, the light, the paintings on the walls. Avram tells him, "I want you to know Shira has never said a bad word about you. Pretty good for an ex-husband, know what I mean?"

So it's all friendly. Shira says, "We'd like to invite you to the wedding. Is that too weird?"

No, he tells them, not at all, he'd be happy to come. "We'll always be family."

Avram offers a blessing over the wine. "I wish we could spend more time together, but I've got work tonight at my place. But soon. Let's go out for dinner."

Now the front door opens and slams. "That must be Gabe," Shira says "We had a little fight on the weekend."

"Kids," Avram says, to make the parents comfortable.

Sam calls, "Gabe? Come in, Gabe, say hello."

"I'm busy. I'm here to do laundry."

"Just for a minute. Okay?" Shira pleads. "Your dad's here."

And Gabe comes in, lugging a bag of dirty clothes. Even angry he's good looking; he's powerfully built, a lot taller than his father, a basketball player. He won't look at them. He stands in the entrance to the living room, leaning against the wall, exuding—and intending to make it damn clear he's exuding—hostility. Does he feel judged or judge today? Sam wonders. Ah, the latter. Gabe knows that both his parents feel guilty when he gets angry; somehow, his anger, as well as what he's angry about, becomes their fault.

Well—and maybe it is. Maybe it is.

"What is it?" Shira asks. "What's all this anger for?"

"As if you didn't know."

"Me, *I* don't know," Sam says. "Explain."

"Just their plans for a grand honeymoon. You know where they're going, Dad? They're going to Israel."

"We have political differences," Shira says. "Do we have to be ugly to each other because of politics?"

"Who's talking politics? I'm talking robbing a people blind. Oppressing them. Taking away their land."

"Gabe, it's *so* much more complicated," Sam says. "I could give you a history lesson, but I know you don't want that. Please. Try to be open to complexities."

"Complexities! Be open to complexities!"

"At least don't insult your mother. And your future stepfather." Sam holds Avram, as it were, in the outstretched palm of his hand, as if introducing him on stage. And now Sam tries to make the quarrel funny. "You know, Avram, our son's a member of some angry group—*Justice for Palestine*. Right, Gabe? A group at B.U."

Avram shakes his head. "This I didn't know. We have had debates about Israel."

"So this group supports BDS at the university," Gabe tells Avram. "That's Boycott, Divestment, and Sanctions. BDS."

"All these initials," Sam says, sighs. "Look—we all want to see peace in Israel, but—"

"Peace! Everybody wants peace, Dad. But suppose 'peace' means the violence of the status quo. My group is made up mostly of Jews. But we want to 'Stop Israeli Apartheid.' That's a slogan," Gabe says. "I know it's simplistic. It's just a slogan."

Stop Israeli Apartheid. This rings a bell for Sam. *Where did I hear it?*

"You have a large group at B.U?" Avram asks.

Gabe shrugs. Doesn't answer.

"Will you please speak to us?"

"All right, all right. So the thing is, we support boycotting Israel. I don't want my friends to find out my own mother and stepfather are going to *honeymoon* in Israel."

"Israelis are your people," Avram says. "They're *our* people."

"Yeah, well . . . ." He puts his bag of clothes down. "You guys," he says to his parents, "you named me Gabriel. I didn't choose it, this name from the Bible. But if I've got it, I've got a right to speak my mind about 'our people,' don't I?"

Gabe picks up his big bag of clothes and storms off to the laundry room. Sam feels embarrassed for Shira in front of Avram. Aach, this son of theirs. To make things a little smoother Sam lifts his glass. "To Israel," he whispers, smiling, as if they shared a secret. He's about to describe to Avram the defacement of the synagogue by some racist sons of bitches when he stops, *remembers.*

Oh, my God.

In mind's eye he sees the weekend spray-painted scrawl: *Stop Israeli Apartheid.* A slogan? It might not be

Gabe who painted the words on the wall. But very likely someone in his group? And here Sam thought he was facing skinheads. But, he says to himself again, haters are haters. Moslem haters, Nazi haters, Jewish haters. Haters on the right, on the left. And a poor kid using ideology as a way of encoding and enacting his anger about the breakup of a family.

Gabe sits in the laundry room reading a newspaper. Sam sticks his head in. "Let me know when you're leaving. I want to walk with you back to B.U."

When the clothes are dry, Gabe barks out, "Leaving."

Sam says goodbye to Shira and Avram. He catches up to Gabe, who's lugging on his back, like a peddler, the green trash bag of folded, clean clothes.

Old snow sits on the slide, the swings, in the playground across the street. A beat-up Chevy, its rear covered with peeling bumper stickers, a sheaf of parking tickets tied to the windshield wipers, has been clamped in a boot. "You went to say Kaddish last week, right?" Gabe asks.

"I wish you'd have come."

"Oh, please!"

Sam gets serious. He puts an arm over Gabe's shoulder and stops them. "Gabe. The police know about your group," he lies. "About your defacement of the synagogue. About the stolen sign."

Gabe shrugs off his father's arm. Sam doesn't look at him but knows Gabe's face is a deadpan. Sam forces himself to say nothing. Finally, finally, Gabe says, "I know. I'm sorry. I believe what I believe about Israel. But what they did—that was so stupid. Dad? I had nothing to do with it. I heard about it later."

"I know that."

"How do you know?"

Sam doesn't explain. Just nods. *Thank God*, he says—to himself. Or to God. Still, the kid *knows* about it, the theft and vandalism. "Here's the thing," Sam says. "I'll cover the costs of the damage, the sign, the removal of paint, and you, when you have the money—maybe years from now—when you have the money and when you're ready to take responsibility for being part of a terrible thing, you can pay me back what you feel is fair."

Gabe is holding back tears, and the more he tries, the more he's crying. "I'm sorry. I'll pay it back. I'll talk to the guys. It's mostly one, two men in the group. They were all puffed up. I've been figuring how to drop out." At the corner a car hits a pot hole of slush and splashes it their way. They back off. "Dad? I'm really, really sorry," Gabe says again.

"You're *better* than this. It's a hate crime, Gabe. They could go to jail. You could go to jail as an accessory. "

"Bennie would never have been a part of something so dumb, right? Anyway—he loved Israel. He talked about joining the IDF."

Sam is silent for almost a block. When they get to Commonwealth and turn toward Kenmore Square, he says, "Do I do that to you? About Bennie? Make him some kind of hero you can't live up to?"

"No. No. Never. Not really."

"I'll walk you to your dorm." It's as if a window has been opened up into their family. He's known and not known. He'd planned to tell Gabe about the synagogue, B'nai Shalom—the enormous differences of opinion on Israel. Just as in the land of Israel itself. Ridiculous to put up a pasteboard picture of your own imagining and call it "Israel" and hate it. Sam understands what Gabe is really hating. Has his anger anything at all to do with politics? He puts his arm over Gabe's shoulder again. Gabe leaves it there.

"I still want to put pressure on Israel. But I will drop out of that group. Really. I'll drop out. Okay?"

"Good . . . . Gabe? You don't think those guys would go further, do you, Gabe?"

"Further? You mean like blow something up? No. No, Dad. Absolutely not. Listen. I wasn't there, Dad. I heard about the painting later. It was really stupid. I know that. Anyway, synagogues aren't the same as Israel. And I know how much it means to you."

"Do you?"

"I mean it takes away your pain."

"You think so, huh?"

"No. Not really. Listen. Maybe I can find out what they did with the sign. Maybe I can even get it back. But my position hasn't changed. Look at the occupation. Look at the humiliation the Palestinians face every day. And the settlements: more and more of them."

Sam could argue, speak about the history of negotiations. About the distorted views of Israel in the press. And — let's face it — about his own ambivalence. His love of Israel, his disagreements with some Israeli policies. And about the synagogue, where, actually, there's no agreement, but everyone wants the best for Israel. Two Jews, three opinions.

Finally, when they're almost at the dorms, again he puts his arm around his son. "I'll talk to Rabbi Stein. It'll be all right. You know, when you were kids, you and Bennie, you were always the one with the complex imagination. You were the one to see all sides of everything. Bennie had such passion, such decisiveness, he was wonderful, but he could be one-sided. I always respected your openness."

"I really miss him."

"I know."

"I miss our family. Dad? It's gone. Bennie. Divorce. All so gone. There is no family."

"I know how you feel. I'm sorry."

"Sorry! You know what? You could have held on. Why didn't you? You could have stuck it out with each other. Imagine what Bennie would have said."

"I'm sorry, Gabe. You know, I *do* imagine."

"Too late now. Too late."

"It is. We went today for a Jewish divorce." Then he

adds, "But you can see, we're kind to each other now."

"It's so goddamn sad," Gabe says, almost sings, having to be heard over the noise of a trolley rising above ground. They're standing now in front of the middle of three giant apartment buildings on Commonwealth Ave — dorms at Boston University. Sam feels wiped out, too cold to stand here in the wind beside a pile of gray slush. But he doesn't want to leave Gabe. He puts his gloved hands on Gabe's cheeks and kisses his forehead. "A blessing," he says. "We both love you. We both trust you. It's a funny kind of family, Gabe, but we're still your parents."

"I've got a paper due." Gabe places his cheek — rough, prickly — against his father's smooth cheek. "Goodnight, Dad." He walks away, turns. "Listen — if you want me to call the rabbi, I will."

"Good. Let me speak to the rabbi first."

Sam starts off for the parking garage. Stops.

Wind whips dust along Commonwealth. He turns his back on the wind, calls Rabbi Stein, puts a message on his machine.

He stands still in the January damp-and-dark. Holding the phone in his gloved hand, he examines it like an instrument of divination. Now, breathing hard, he calls Shira, and for the seven, eight seconds the phone rings tells himself he should hang up.

"It's Sam. Is Avram with you?"

"No. He had to work at his place, remember? Why?"

"Can I stop by a minute?"

Walking to Shira's he tries to formulate what he wants to say. He revises and revises, as if it were a speech.

He buzzes, she buzzes back to let him in. The empty champagne bottle and glasses are gone from the coffee table. She's wearing slippers and her blue house robe. She waves him to her wing-backed chair and sits across from him on the couch, as if this were an interview. He knows from the way she sits, self conscious, in angular relaxation, as well as where she's decided to seat them, that even after the Jewish divorce and their odd closeness, after his friendliness with Avram, she feels discomfort. Maybe about Gabe? Or is she simply mirroring his own discomfort?

At this moment, he realizes, separate from himself, an observer, that he doesn't intend to tell her about Gabe, about the defacement of the synagogue. Don't her rights as a mother trump Gabe's rights to privacy? And if not to tell her, what is he doing here?

He hears himself begin.

"It's going to sound funny. But our divorce today has made me aware of *us* — us as a couple, our peculiar ending these past two years. And today."

"But you can see," she says, "it's not an ending, is it? Here we are."

"No. It's not. But I've been thinking about Gabe."

"What did he say to you?" she asks.

He doesn't reply. To soothe himself, he rubs his hand

over the cream-colored velvet of the armrest. So peculiar. How long have they known each other — over twenty-five years. And he actually feels shy, awkward. It would be so much better if they were sitting together on the couch.

"You've been thinking about Gabe," she prompts. "And?"

"About Gabe, and about today's divorce, and it got me wondering if — don't laugh — we should consider — even at this late date — consider being together. Being a family again for Gabe."

"Oh, Sam. Look at the way you asked. You're not even thinking about *us*. You're thinking about Gabe." She gets up, comes over to him, leans down, and runs her fingers through his thinning hair.

"I said it stupidly," he says.

"You did, dear. With a good heart. For Gabe. We both love him so much." Sitting next to him on a corner of his chair, she says, "But you and me, Sam? Maybe we can have a friendship. I'm sure we can. But you don't want me. I'm with Avram. And Gabe — Gabe will be all right. Don't you think?"

"He's not all right."

"He's unhappy?"

Sam doesn't answer this. "I like Avram. He'll be a good man for you."

She kisses him on the cheek. He holds her arms in his big hands, keeps her off, refuses this kind of kiss.

He finds himself on the street. What was he saying?
If there's anyone he wants, really wants, it's Kate Schiff,
Kate from morning minyan. He hardly knows her. But
she's the woman he thinks about, sees in mind's eye when
he wakes in the middle of the night. He runs the fingers of
his soul through Kate's soft, light brown hair. Yet look! —
he offered himself to Shira! Of course she refused — of
course she refused. Didn't he know she'd refuse? How
could it have worked? What kind of fool is he?

At once he's flooded by Kate's gentle face. He thinks
of phoning her. From foolishness to foolishness. Nineteen
years between them!

Still, he fingers his phone in his pocket.

But it's too late at night to call. And what can he say?

In the time he was at Shira's it has begun to snow.
Snow covering snow. He walks cautiously now that he
can't see patches of ice. In the ten minutes it takes him to
walk back to the parking garage, more than an inch has
accumulated. Snow fringes stoops, lampposts, parked
cars. The streets have begun to turn white; sewer grates
and iron manhole covers are starkly bare and wet black.
On Commonwealth he hugs the buildings till he gets to
the garage. He'll drive home.

But as if someone else were in charge, the car doesn't
turn for home. In five, six minutes he's at B'nai Shalom.
Already the temporary sign is slightly warped — they
must have laminated only one side of the cardboard.

His key slips easily into the lock and turns. Stephanie

oiled it since last Tuesday. It's an empty shul. There were adult ed classes here tonight, finished now, but the shul is still warm. It's dark except for security lights. He passes the library and large sanctuary and unlocks the door to the small sanctuary. At its entrance he takes a yarmulke from the basket and stands facing the ark. The only light is the little bulb over the ark. Alone, standing in the near-dark without a prayer book, for a congregation of one he recites the Shema and then, skipping most of the evening service, whispers prayers for his son's healing and whispers the *Hashkivenu: Help us to lie down in peace. . . . Spread over us the shelter of Your peace.* At once he realizes: that prayer is the reason he's here—as if the words, in Hebrew, could act as a magic formula to draw peace his way, Gabe's way.

In the near-dark he whispers, *Help us be at peace. Yes. Help Gabe. Help me be a better father. Help Gabe and me, help Gabe and his mother.*

Then he adds: *If it be Your will, let me know love again.*

Time to sleep. Time to go home and sleep. Eleven o'clock. It's almost Tuesday. A few more hours and, Kate Schiff standing behind him, he'll be here again, first thing in the morning, chanting prayers.

* * *

Children of Peace

TUESDAY MORNING, the synagogue still dark. Locking the car, Kate looks up at the old, red brick building, once, a hundred years ago, a home for a wealthy family. She feels a little sick to her stomach when, again, she sees the temporary sign—makeshift on paper laminated over cardboard, in place of the stolen sign. *B'nai Shalom*. Children of Peace. The temporary sign contradicts its words: for the original, simple professional sign, urethaned, carved in maple, was stolen a couple of weeks ago; graffiti on the synagogue wall, now sand blasted off, cursed Israel. Last week the local giveaway weekly newspaper gave the vandalism a lot of space. Children of *Peace*? Whatever peace she finds here will be the peace she brings with her, and today that's not much.

As usual, she's the second congregant for the Tuesday morning minyan. Only Sam Schulman is present so far in the small sanctuary for the Tuesday morning minyan, his blue and white full body tallis covering him like resting wings, tefillin strapped to his arm and above his forehead. In gray light from the clearstory windows Kate sees those little hard leather boxes, attached by leather straps, not as containers for holy words, which is what they are, but as conduits of spiritual energy. Traditionally, women didn't strap them on; but why shouldn't they? She'd like to wear tefillin, especially now, whatever the Orthodox say. Like the synagogue itself, she's unaffiliated. Just a Jew, a convert. Nobody would mind. And she can do with some holy energy.

In the absence of other congregants Sam has begun chanting morning prayers, rocking a little to their rhythm. Last week, Kate remembers, Sam recited Mourners' Kaddish for his older son, two years gone. She, too, has a son, so precious to her; she can imagine what Sam has gone through. She felt Sam's loss last Tuesday almost as if she were a second mourner.

Balding, Sam, a long, strong face, clean shaven. A big man. Not conventionally handsome like Mark, her ex. She likes his face, Sam's face. He's a tall, broad man, physically powerful. She imagines his strength as a symbol of moral strength, though of course she knows the two are unrelated. In her mind it's as if carrying his son's death, a burden to lift daily, has strengthened him morally, the way lifting weights gives physical strength.

Hearing her come in, without turning or stopping, Sam nods his head. Kate puts a small tallis over her shoulders and begins murmuring with him.

At the end of a blessing he stops, turns to her. "Before everyone else comes, tell me — what did the court say?"

Yesterday "the court" — in fact, not a judge but a kind young social worker, aide to the clerk magistrate — talked to Kate while Danny cooled his heels in the waiting room. "You don't want Danny to end up with a record," Ms. Bennett said. "At fourteen? But before we can drop charges, we need to know he's acceding to the treatment plan he's given. That includes doing therapy if the court so mandates. And Mrs. Schiff? If I were you, I'd be concerned about his attitude."

Kate hears her mother, knows she hears her, pointing out yet again Kate's failures as Danny's mother. But Ms. Bennett is different, is trying to be kind, looking for signs of accommodation. She'll give them to her.

"Well, you know," Kate said, "he goes to a good school, and he gets straight A's. He's a strong student. Lately he's made these terrible friends." She'd already let Ms. Bennett know, as if casually, that she has all sorts of credentials of respectability. She was ashamed to do this; it was cheap, degrading, vulgar. But she did it.

"That's fine, Mrs. Schiff. But when I tried to speak to your son, he wouldn't look me in the face. Here's the thing—we don't expect some make-believe repentance, but we want to see a reasonable, respectful attitude. He messed up. Okay? '*I messed up. It won't happen again.*' That's all. But if the clerk magistrate sees sourness, hostility, arrogance—well, frankly, what happens here isn't fixed in stone, Mrs. Schiff. He might well be arraigned. It depends on your boy."

"Absolutely. I'll talk to him like a Dutch uncle." Looking at the woman's face, she realized "Dutch uncle" was meaningless to Ms. Bennett.

Kate sat next to Danny, evaluated his expression, and forced a smile. Skinny kid, still small. He's like a puppy with the big feet that let you know he's going to grow. In fact Danny's just begun a growth spurt. She ran her fingers through his wild-man, half-dreadlocks, hair. He pretended to her—and to himself—that he minded, and pulled away. Yes, he did look sour, looked almost convincingly hostile and arrogant.

"Dan? Danny?" For the court he needed—though she wouldn't put it to him this way—to eat crow, to express remorse. And the thing is, the boy *felt* remorse. The hostility, the surly swagger, the dead-eyed cool—all were cover for his shame. A stolen wristwatch in his pocket? *Guilty.* A little bag of marijuana? *Guilty.* And of stunning stupidity: *guilty*—to shoplift on a dare and with drugs in his pocket!

He dressed for the court as if he were going to synagogue, but if she hadn't demanded, he'd have worn torn jeans and a tee shirt. She wanted this to end in real change, not in humiliation. The court mandated: he was going to be kept out of Harvard Square for six months—"except when with his parents." Meaning just Kate, since Mark, his father, the rat, is working at his own bio-tech something or other in Hawaii—where his new wife is from.

This requirement—to stay out of Harvard Square—was actually a gift to Danny as well as Kate; though he groaned, she was sure he was in fact relieved—it didn't have to be *his choice*, his renunciation, staying away from the cool kids who hung near the subway kiosk and the hamburger place.

And really, she tells Sam this morning in the small sanctuary—when Danny's with those kids, all older, they get crazy together. The shoplifting was just a dare, a challenge, she tells him. They literally ran through the store—no style, no strategy, grab, pocket, and out again. A wilding. Danny, last boy out the door, got caught.

"I know what it's like," Sam says when she tells him in a few words what happened at court. "Listen. My boy, my son at B.U., he has in fact been part of some very dumb things, too." He turns, is about to say more, but instead makes a pocket of his two hands, and for a few seconds captures Kate's hand in sympathy. It comforts them both. Now the Breitbarts come in and Amy, the Hebrew school teacher, her six-month old baby in a sling, and Sam returns to davening. In a few minutes they're short only one congregant, and soon Nick Shorr, Executive Director of the synagogue, is present. Now they have a full minyan and can chant Kaddish and the Barekhu.

At the end of morning service, Kate asks him quietly, "Sam? Can you come over to my place tonight? I'll be too busy to cook but we can share a couple of pizzas, the three of us. Okay? Frankly, I'd like you to talk privately to Danny. Not to advise. To listen to him. I think he can be helped by a man, listening. A man he respects. He respects you."

He smiles, he nods. He asks no questions. "Of course. What time?"

It's the first time they've ever been anything but synagogue buddies.

Now she's off to Tufts, where she coordinates an aspect of the STEM programs—Science, Technology, Engineering and Mathematics. God knows she'd never imagined she'd become an administrator. Let alone that she'd like it. But she's so busy. All day she runs, she runs. Meeting to conference to telephone call. Taking yesterday morning off to go to court with Danny, then talk to him and bring him to school, means that today she has to squeeze in even more than usual. But she can't skip the morning minyan—especially because Sam is prayer leader.

Tonight Kate finds Danny already home from school. And he's set the table for three—she'd texted him that Sam Schulman would be here. That Danny came home early and actually set the table—these are very, very good signs. Putting down her laptop case, she kisses Danny's forehead and straightens the livingroom, placing all the embroidered pillows diagonally at the corners of the couch. She remembers Mark making fun of her for buying those pillows. And that glass-fronted bookcase— she found it in an antique shop, slightly damaged, for practically nothing. This is a gracious house, furnished gracefully, each piece chosen with love — a beautiful, old-fashioned house in Brookline, Edwardian, 1908, that's been very well kept up. The living room has stained wainscoting, ship-lapped, a bay window that daytime offers a wash of light. Now, late January, it's dark out. She pulls the drapes across the darkness and lights little candles everywhere.

The solid, expensive furniture comes from when they were a family, a well-heeled family. The house is so much bigger and more elegant than she and Danny need; Mark ceded her the house when he left, but it's up to her to pay the mortgage. And that's been hard. And hard to pay for heat; she's closed off more than half the house. She's always on Danny's case: *turn out lights when you leave a room.* Sometimes, when Danny's not home, she steps into one of the unused rooms, and for a moment she's back in her old life. It's like a flashback in a movie. She imagines the room clean — she used to have a cleaning person in once a week. At first, for a few moments, she doesn't see the dust, doesn't feel the chill, half-sees Mark at his desk working on his laptop, or, in another room, bare, so bare, imagines Mark's barbells and rowing machine — all the things she sold on Craigslist last winter.

Mark pays child support — but less than any court would mandate. This was her fault. As her mother tells her again and again over the phone, all she had to do was demand. But she didn't want to see herself as one of those greedy, hostile women. What a snob she's been, pretending to some kind of phony aristocratic grace. So fast, the way her life (and therefore Danny's life) has slipped, until it's inches from the edge. Every day she says, *Tomorrow I'll have to put the house on the market and get out from under the mortgage and look for a small apartment.*

Most of the furniture will have to be sold or stored. How she'll hate to lose this.

She slides the two pizzas into the oven, puts together a salad, opens a bottle of wine. And here's Sam at the door. Danny knows Sam only a little. Sam helped him shape his Torah talk, his *d'var Torah*, for his Bar Mitzvah last year. And it was Sam who, on behalf of the synagogue board, handed Danny the prayer book and Kiddush cup. Danny is very formal with him, calls him "Professor Schulman," calls him "sir." Calls almost nobody "sir." Kate gives Sam a quick hug and goes off to the kitchen so Sam will have a chance to talk with Danny privately.

She hears only fragments. But enough. Hears mostly Danny, whose voice, high-pitched though broken, can be made out from one end of the house to the other. She hears an evenness of tone. Neither one excited. Neither one angry or trying to talk over the other. Though it will dry out the pizza, she keeps the oven temperature low to give them time. When she calls "Pizza, gentlemen," Sam calls back, "One minute, okay?" And then it's five minutes. More. So what? Let the pizza dry out.

After dinner, Danny goes to his room to do homework.

Kate stops him at the foot of the stairs. "Good conversation, honey?" He shrugs. "Yeah, actually."

Returning to Sam, she whispers, "That seemed to go well. You don't need to tell me what you talked about."

"Nothing very secret. I think it went well. Yes. Suppose I take him on as something of a project. This sounds stupid—but I mean, be a kind of uncle."

Tears well up. "Why should that sound stupid? *Thank* you."

"Danny's a real good kid. I like your son. I like him a lot." Without asking, he fills her glass with wine and sits beside her on the couch. Now, surprising her, he puts his arm around her and, smiling, squeezes. As older brother or uncle? As father? As comforter? As lover? She knows very well. She leaves the arm but shakes her head. He doesn't argue. But sighs.

She says, "We're both serious people, Sam."

"What does that mean?"

She doesn't say.

"I know. I'm so much older than you. I know that."

Yes, you are. Nineteen years older, in fact. And what is she supposed to say?—*Oh, years don't matter. The gap doesn't matter.* But sure it matters. She in her mid thirties, he in his mid fifties. She just born when he graduated college. If they get together, if they stay together—she's already thinking that far ahead!—when she's sixty he'll be almost eighty. Still, she realizes they're already in the midst of checking each other out. Knows all at once she asked him over as much for herself as for Danny. Those aren't separate. She's recruiting (God help her—to be that foolish!) a family savior. Is that it?

Sam encourages her to feel held. He offers both her and Danny a grounding—a solid male presence. Yes, exactly. Well? She's not ashamed of that. And this sense of being held—bolstered, supported—let's face it, it makes her feel how shaky her ordinary single self really is. She feels often, especially at night, that she inhabits the Country of Chaos—or that chaos inhabits her. Strange: at work she continues to be efficient and creative. Chaos enters when she's alone, or when Danny's in another room and she, she's supposed to be holding the fort.

And she's afraid—afraid as if this were the middle of a wilderness. As if they were surrounded by savages and the fort isn't all that secure.

It's as if Sam might offer protection and order, take her hand and (a change of metaphors) lay down a clear grid over her too-fluid life, offer boundaries, offer a story to compose of her life instead of a hodgepodge of *copings*. When she talks to him—on a Saturday morning after services, say—she can feel herself enter a sensible world. Of course it's *his* world, but she doesn't mind that.

It's odd to think that *structure, order,* can feel, well, erotic.

"I'm wondering," he says, changing the subject, "if Danny might like to shoot hoops some evening. I think my son Gabe can slip Danny into the gym at B.U."

"Sure. I know he'd love that. If he has time. He's on his junior high team."

"It'd be good for Gabe, too. I'll explain sometime."

Now they don't speak. She collects the dishes and silverware, brings them to the sink; he loads the dishwasher. At length she says, "And maybe . . ." (as if this followed logically from his suggestion) "we can meet for coffee sometime without Danny."

It's a Thursday, an evening without Danny, who's playing pickup basketball with Gabe. It's worked out. Sam didn't have to twist his son's arm, he tells Kate, to get him to pick up Danny, take him to the gym. "Gabe feels he owes me. He got involved with some arrogant students. A club. They were self-righteous—they were damn foolish. Worse than that. Gabe himself didn't do anything terrible, but the group did. And he knew something about it."

"Don't think you have to tell me."

"Of course it has to stay private. But since he's with Danny, I think you ought to know: The group is "Justice for Palestine"—a couple of them stole the synagogue sign and defaced the wall with swastikas and hate words. Ironically, they're mostly Jews. Full of half-baked ideology. The group protests Israel's occupation of the West Bank. Ultimately, they want peace. Some stupid way to bring about peace. Gabe knew something about it. He didn't do it but he knew. He's left the group. We got the sign back a couple of days ago. And they made a deal with the rabbi. They'll replant the sign and pay what it cost to erase the marks."

"Gabe is such a good young man."

"He is. He made a big mistake. He's okay. He's making changes."

Sam had suggested they meet for a drink on Commonwealth, but as he was driving to meet her she called and said, "Sam? Why don't you just come over to my place?"

Now a bottle of wine sits almost full on the coffee table in the empty living room. They don't finish a single glass before he draws her shoulders into his thick hands. She presses toward him, gives herself to those big hands of his, and he stands with her and kisses her, long, long. She leads him to her bedroom. Her mother's photo is on her night table; in a comic gesture — she herself the audience — she turns her mother's face toward the wall.

Now Sam and Kate lie naked under her covers looking into each other's eyes and touching, stroking. Everywhere he touches wakes her. "This," he says, "is so beautiful."

"Yes."

"Kate, listen Kate, I've been wanting you since I first saw you."

She rehearses beautiful things to say back to him, but ends by nodding and burrowing her head into his big chest.

Having undressed slowly, now they make love

slowly. Oh, very sweet. She's left brimming with desire, desire all over. Now he begins to kiss her body, as if there were lips everywhere. So gentle! It's like a meditation. And when he enters her again she opens to him, consciously *lets* herself open, and it's as if she were all permeable, her skin transparent, so that it's not just her sex taking him in, moving with him. All of her is flowering, it's as if they're growing something together, blooming together, and it becomes grander and grander, until she bursts, and he holds back, now starts again and she comes more deeply and more fully and keeps flowing out. He joins her, they cry out, trying to be quiet, and she whispers, *Sam, shh, the people next door* . . . .

He kisses her.

She finds herself crying.

She apologizes for the tears: "It happens sometimes. Really, Sam, it's a good crying."

By the time Danny and Gabe are home, Sam and Kate have washed and dressed and look like respectable adults having a glass of wine with dinner. Gabe heads back to B.U.; Danny sits at the table with them and Sam pours him a very little wine. "They actually let me play," Danny says, his voice rising and falling. "You know—a pick-up game. Some of the guys I could fake right around. Like this." He demonstrates. "I actually did okay. I'm not great, and those guys were a lot bigger—but I'm fast. At first they let me get around them. Then they tried to stop me for real. Then Gabe and I went out for Chinese."

Kate knows Danny; she can hear him play Excited Child. It's kind of a role, kind of a fake, pretended innocence, a cover. Why? Is he nervous about Sam? Does he know something's happened? He's friendly but he doesn't look straight at Sam. *Is it that obvious?* Or is she the one feeling uneasy and projecting her unease onto Danny?

Already she's imagining life within Sam's story: life in a traditional family, meaning a family that respects traditions, with a strong, loving father — well . . . *step*father — who can bring a traditional life, a Jewish life, to the table. She imagines sharing a Seder with Sam and their two boys at Passover. She imagines imbibing from him a heritage she didn't grow up with.

A few years ago, she would have been ashamed to give over any of her authority, her power, her work of self-creation, to any tradition or any person. When she married Mark, yes, she converted and even took Mark's name: Schiff. But at first nothing changed; she simply went from secular Christian to nominal Jew. It didn't mean much to Mark. He was busy "growing the business," seven days a week; she began attending Shabbat services while Danny was in Saturday Hebrew school. Then, slowly, especially when Mark was preparing to leave and Danny was studying to become a Bar Mitzvah, she took it upon herself to learn to chant Torah, though she barely knew what the words meant and it took her hours to learn a few lines.

Last October, for the festival of Sukkot, a year after Mark left, she and Danny built their first-ever sukkah, an open shelter of 2 x 4's bolted together, walled in fabric — a structure commanded in Torah, a shelter defined in Talmud, through whose "roof" — strips of burlap — one can see the stars. And surprise — it didn't fall down. They ate some of their meals in the sukkah. As commanded.

It isn't that she wants to give up all her responsibility for making a life. But she wants to enter the dance with a pre-existing choreography — as she has begun to enter. What's self-deprecating about that? So what if it's not a dance she was the one to choreograph. Do we each have to be Huck Finn lighting out for the territories? Abraham may be a better model; God instructs: *Go, go, take yourself from your father's house and from your native land to the land that I will show you.*

That I will show you makes all the difference. Sam isn't Abraham; she's not Sarah. But maybe both of them can live according to one beautiful paradigm.

Sam's looking at a photograph of Danny, a framed photograph on Kate's desk. Danny's at an away game; so they have a rare few hours alone together. "I know we have to take it slow," Sam says, pointing to the picture, meaning Danny, considering Danny.

When Danny's home, Sam's been stopping by, simply like a new, good friend, every few days. He brings take-out or he comes for Kate's soup. Brings a video or watches a basketball game with Danny. She admires his simple strategy and loves it that he's willing to consider a strategy at all. Loves it that in the middle of a busy school week, when he has to prepare to teach modern novel at B.U. the next day, he takes off the time to be with them. Or meets them on a Sunday afternoon to skate at Lars Anderson Park.

And when he comes over, miraculously Danny settles down, doesn't balk, doesn't become his sometimes-snotty self. He becomes serious. Or childlike. Or a pretend adult. You'd never know what he can sometimes be like. A teen-age monster. For there are times, oh, yes, when she can't do anything right; Doesn't that fruit belong in the *fridge*, Mom? Or do you *want* it to get rotten? Why don't you sometimes, once in a while, close the doors of the cup-board? — I'm always closing them (*slam, slam*). I hate that brand — I told you, right? Do you *have* to tell me when to do my homework? God, Mom, you can be so annoying.

Oh, she loves him dearly, even at his worst, even when at the same time she's angry at him; she feels that honestly it's her fault when he gets mean or snotty. She has never been firm enough — even before his father left. And now, she knows, Danny's taking that departure out on her.

When Mark calls, Danny is "too busy to talk." Mark wants Danny to fly to Hawaii next summer. Kate, not wanting to get between them, hands Danny the phone. She hears him grunt, not answer. He slams down the receiver and says, "That bastard thinks he can just whistle and I'll come. Well I won't. He can go screw himself."

"You're making a mistake," she says. "He *is* your father," she says, setting herself up for eye-rolling. "You loved him. It wasn't you he was leaving. You know that. Maybe you should think about it. You really want to lose your father? You'd be cutting off a part of yourself."

"You and your big psychology! I should spend a month with him and his babe? Yeah, right—you know when? When he gets a court order."

"He won't, Danny. You know that."

"Well, good. Great."

She feels a kind of ugly delight well up. *That bastard deserves it.* She resists the feeling.

Danny is vaguely aware of his mother and Sam, their relationship. Yesterday he said, "You don't have to pretend, Mom. About Sam. It's okay with me, I mean, if you're kind of romantic. He's cool." He may be cool, Sam, but what's wonderful about Sam is that he doesn't act "cool." In fact, he doesn't act. He has no style; he wears old wool sweaters full of pilling, which he removes, God help us, with duct tape or Mark's old left-behind electric razor. Sam manifests humility—a humility with strength. He doesn't placate Danny or challenge Danny, and Danny doesn't challenge him. For awhile during the gray dregs of winter Kate thinks maybe it's going to be easy.

No such luck.

The snow has melted, the days are warmer. Kate is working hard with students who have been accepted at Tufts for next fall, students interested in Science, Technology, Engineering or Mathematics. It's hard to find time to be with Sam. There have been a couple of sweet evenings when Danny's hanging out with a friend. She's been hiding her sexuality from her son as she once hid it from her parents.

Then comes a Saturday when Danny's playing an away game. She takes him to school, where the minibus and a few family cars will be starting from. A gray day, a light drizzle. She's excited: she goes to synagogue — only half an hour late — and sits with Sam. After services, not staying for the blessings over the wine and bread, the nosh and schmooze, they slip away, breathless, filled with tenderness; his car follows hers back to her house.

The rain is a little heavier, but they're wrapped up in each other, squirrel in under her sheets and make love, slowly, slowly. And afterwards, he whispers, "This is what a Shabbat should be." She doesn't say, but she feels, *Yes, yes. The afternoon is generating holy love, Shabbos love.* She presses her cheek against his, collects the warmth, draws it into her. They fall into a Shabbos nap.

How could they have guessed that the roof of the gym in Wellesley would be leaking so badly that the game would have to be canceled — that they'd hear the buzzer, then the click of a key in the front door lock and bolt up, both of them, out of bed.

"Mom?"

They're into their outer clothes in a few moments;

the clothes they don't have time for, their underwear, gets kicked into the bedroom closet. She straightens her blouse, runs her fingers through Sam's thin hair—it doesn't help make him more respectable—and they call out, "Hi, Danny! Hi! Ah, you're home!" He stands at her bedroom door and doesn't look at either of them. Looks at the crumpled bed, pastes on a smile, and backs away. "See—big leak in the gym roof. The rain poured in like you wouldn't believe. Tony's mom drove me home."

"Want hot chocolate, Danny?"

"No. Uh uh. No, thanks."

Why should Danny be so disturbed when he already knew that they were "romantic"? Dumb question. She gets it, she gets it. A man not your father, even a man you respect, in your mother's bedroom? Knowing, and facing it almost head-on—oh, they're different, so different— romance and sex.

Sadly, *Danny's* different. Maybe it's their expectation of difference that changes him, expectation of his unease that makes him uneasy. They must act differently, too. Is he attuned to their embarrassment? Whatever's going on—he's distant this afternoon, and they're distant—and more awkward. When Danny's off in his own room, Sam says, with regret, "I'm afraid it's going to take a while for things to get easy again."

Sunday, she thinks, should help. Gabe has gotten him and Dan into a kind of demonstration and master class with a Celtics player, Courtney Lee. Is Gabe's kindness a sort of payback to his father? She supposes it is. But he seems to really like Danny. Danny hasn't been able to talk about anything else all week.

But Sunday morning Danny's moody; he snaps at her. "Your *boy*friend coming over?" he asks, extending *boy*, making Sam into a joke or worse—something nasty. She snaps back, "Listen, Danny. You got a problem? You stop taking it out on me. I'm doing my best, goddamnit."

"Look at you. He's so *ancient*," Danny says. "You're robbing the old age home."

Nasty—but comic. She wants to slap his face. She knows that the comedy is meant to lighten his challenge. Still, her anger has been building—she forgives and placates too much till now she's had it. It's happened before. "You go to your room until you can live with me like a civil person! I expect respect from you!" Though in fact, let's be straight here—she doesn't *expect* respect. Quite the opposite. She just prays for it. Mornings (except for Tuesday at minyan) she says only a few prayers—prayers in her own words—but always the prayers include a petition that she be a good mother to Danny, that she stand up to his blows, and that he recognize how much she tries, that he value her.

Then Sunday at lunch, while they're waiting for Gabe, Danny won't talk to her. Won't look at her. And now, as if simple distance isn't sufficient punishment, he changes his mind about the afternoon. "You know what? I've got to go do some homework." He goes for his raincoat.

Somehow he feels he's won points in their battle.

"But what about Gabe? The basketball class!" she says. "Gabe worked hard to get you in. He's coming for you. Danny!"

"You just want me out of the house so your boyfriend can come over. Well, don't worry — I'm going. " He stops. "But tell Gabe I'm sorry."

And Danny's out the door. She expects he'll cool down and call, even if only to put her down for something. That's standard when he's mad. She steels herself for the call, understanding what it will really be about. But by the time Sam and Gabe arrive, he still hasn't called.

Sam says to Gabe, "Sorry. I know you went out of your way."

Gabe shrugs. "He's a kid. It's okay. I'll go anyway. It's a cool thing. To watch a guy make those moves?"

"Sure, but it's really not okay," Sam says. He takes Gabe's arm. "Come into the living room with me. More going on than you know. Let me fill you in."

And Kate retreats to the kitchen. She can't hear much of what they say, especially over the hum of the fridge and the snap of her knife chopping onions. It's more the tone she picks up. She knows that Sam is telling Gabe about yesterday, telling him delicately. What about Gabe? she wonders. Will *he* get upset, too? She hears, ". . . acting out. . ." She hears, ". . . stupid of us. . ." Now Sam calls out, "Kate?" and she comes in, apron bowed in back. She feels like an embarrassed teen, but unlike a teen, she can calm herself down and smile. It was so much harder facing Danny.

Sam says, "Gabe doesn't think he went off to a friend's house to study."

Gabe says, "Dad told me about the trouble Danny got into. I'm wondering, you know, like, you think he might be going back to see his old friends? Where d'you think they might be?"

"Oh, my God," she says. "You're right. He's gone back to Harvard Square."

"Where he's not allowed," Sam says to Gabe. "*Because* he's not allowed. If he's picked up, he could get placed in juvenile detention."

Kate undoes the bow on her apron. Sam says, "We'll both go."

And Gabe says, "Me, too. I'll go, too, Dad. Danny wouldn't do so good in juvenile detention."

"Oh, my God," Kate says and puts on her raincoat. "Oh, please God."

They take Sam's car, drive across the river and into Harvard Square. A miserable, gray day. Not likely that Danny would stay on the streets in this weather; still, Sam is going to drive around the area looking while Kate and Gabe split up on foot.

Every few minutes one of them calls another. Anything? Nothing. Kate looks through the Harvard Bookstore, where Danny used to like to browse. And the Chinese restaurant. And *Au Bon Pain*. The Harvard

Coop—its bookstore. Its café. The clothing store in the main building. Everywhere, she shows staff a photo from her wallet. Nobody remembers seeing him. In the Coop she spots Gabe searching. Kate phones him across the main floor. "Gabe?—I'm going to check out the Charles Hotel."

On the way she spots three, four of the kids Danny used to hang with. No Danny. She's thankful. But she's beginning to feel panic, as if Danny had decided to run off to Hawaii somehow. She rushes down Eliot Street to the Charles Hotel and looks through the elegant lobby. Sometimes he used to go there to read. Sam calls her. "Any sign of him?" Then a call from Gabe. "I've found him, Kate. I'm at the Coop. Better come right away."

She hurries back to the Coop. Danny's standing by the cafe next to Gabe and a powerfully built young man in a cheap suit. A store detective? The man's hand rests on Danny's shoulder. A paternal hand? A controlling hand? "Please—what's going on?" she asks, as if simply for information. Her heart is beating a mile a minute.

"Danny was just doing homework in the café," Gabe says—"working on his laptop. Someone spotted him—a manager—he had photos of kids who aren't allowed in the Coop. There was Danny. So the manager called the police. Right, Detective?" Gabe says. "But listen," he says, offering this with open palm. "He's *allowed* to be here with family. Right? So? This is his mother. Okay? And I'm his brother—his stepbrother. I was just the other side of the store a few minutes. It's my fault, not my brother's."

My brother's. A pang goes through Kate.

The detective, who works with juveniles, says, "Okay. Okay, folks. No problem. But you better take him out of here." And they call Sam, he circles and meets them out front. All this time Danny hasn't spoken. He mumbles "Thanks" to the detective. That's all. But in the car, he says thanks to Gabe. And says, "Sorry, Gabe. I don't know. I was just bummed out."

Kate says, "But Harvard Square. What were you doing in Harvard Square. You want to go to a reformatory? You really want that?"

Danny seems to ignore her. But he doesn't seem angry or depressed now. Then he says to Sam, "You know what? Gabe called me 'brother.' Wow. Hey, Gabe. Hey, bro."

Gabe laughs, Sam laughs, but Sam wasn't in the store, and so Kate's sure Sam doesn't get it. Kate explains: "He could only be there with a parent, but the detective let it slide, partly because he was there with a *brother*."

"A brother!" Sam says. "That's great, really great, Gabe. Your saying that. Just great! A family, huh?"

Kate's sitting in the back of the Camry with Danny; Gabe of the long legs is sitting beside his father up front. Right away she understands by the exaggeration in Sam's voice that, yes, it's great. . . but also not so great. It makes him a little uneasy. The man feels caught. She knows, yes, he wants to be caught by her. She sees, when he turns his head slightly, that his eyes are glowing with tears. Can you imagine! But isn't he scared, too?

And is she sure she wants to catch him? To catch this man? *This man,* she keeps saying. He's still strange to her. Increasingly strange. But how good they might be together. She and this man. This family.

It's as if their sons were their parents, their parents acting as marriage brokers. She and Sam are being railroaded into marriage by their own children! It's comic. Someday the boys will find it comic. Not now. The process of courting is being madly speeded up. It's a fast train. Oh, my God. This man—I'm going to actually *marry* him. She looks at him as if examining a stranger. She feels more than a little scared deep in her heart. And, yes, glowing, radiant.

It's another Tuesday morning, another minyan. The synagogue sign has been replanted, its wooden legs replaced with steel and bolted onto Sonotubes. They're still living apart, sleeping apart, Kate and Sam; they arrive at the sanctuary separately. He's there, alone, when she comes in. The others will be there soon. Sam is in front of the closed ark in full-body tallis, davening. He turns to smile at her. Kate covers herself in her smaller tallis and takes up his chant.

* * *

O'Malley Recites
the Kaddish

LAURA O'MALLEY is the most surprising congregant in the Tuesday morning minyan at B'nai Shalom — Children of Peace. For one thing, she's still in college, a half or a third the age of other regulars. For another, well, is she Jewish at all? Red-blonde hair, blue-eyed, she looks like an O'Malley. And while her mother was born Jewish, the O'Malley household was neither Jewish nor Christian. Laura grew up in a family, not of atheists nor even agnostics, but simply of secularists, materialists, for whom the question of God didn't exist. Or was other people's question. They were too polite to say so to friends, but they wondered at the simpletons who believe ridiculous things.

They believe in truth. The "real" world. Laura has always agreed.

This is one of the only ways Laura's mother and father do agree. Another is about how unfair the other spouse is. And another is about Laura's schooling.

Laura is first in her family to go to college as she was first to go to a good prep school. Both on scholarship. Almost full scholarship at Andover, a music scholarship and an "attractive" financial package at Boston University. It's not enough; she's taken out a loan, but it's only a small loan. Her parents won't help. If she studied nursing like Laura's mother, they might feel it worthwhile to take out a loan. But Laura wants to study music, art, and literature. She wants to be a singer.

Laura's father manages one of a chain of stores selling outdoor clothing. He's not rich, but he's proud of what he's done with himself. His father worked in a factory. He wants their only child to be an even bigger success. "A singer?" he says — says again and again. "You think we'll pay for you to sing better? You sing just fine."

This semester, spring semester, she'll work part-time for a home care agency — paid ultimately by the Commonwealth of Massachusetts — drive to Newton, pick up an old, sickly woman, victim of a stroke that cleaved her in two, and drive her in the woman's own wheelchair-accessible van to a synagogue in Brookline for Saturday morning services. "Well," Laura's mother said, "it's a good thing, sweetie. It's *real*, you know what I mean? All your father cares about is the money. But you're doing good for somebody. Better than doing bad for somebody — grilling burgers at that dreadful fast-food place." Which is what Laura did between her first and second years of college, then first semester this year, until she became totally nauseated by the stink of cooked cow.

Before she starts working for Mrs. Kahn, she imagines a Sweet Old Lady, her hands a little shaky, poor old lady, a widow, religious, very dear. She's prepared to love her. Laura's template is her own grandmother, her mother's mother, who died when Laura was eleven. Laura loved Binnie completely, *Binnie* she called her. She massaged Binnie's feet and legs to help the circulation, listened to stories about her grandmother's own grandmother. It was wonderful to go back and back through stories into the nineteenth century, into immigration from Poland, hardship in Chicago. Binnie was a storyteller.

But Mrs. Kahn is not, it turns out, at all like Binnie. Not at all. Anything but.

It's the first Saturday morning; Laura drives up to a small ranch built in the 1950s. A van sits in the driveway. House with vinyl siding, garage a storage room, breezeway between. A house in good condition. Through the glass upper half of the door Laura sees the old lady sitting high, queenly, in her wheelchair — one side paralyzed from the stroke — confronting the kitchen door. Laura knocks and, past tied-back curtains, sees a bulldog face, mouth twisted down at one corner, a hand waving her in with a quick snap! Snap! — as if the woman were splashing water on herself.

"Well it's about time, damnit!"

"Is there a misunderstanding? Actually, Mrs. Kahn, I'm here fifteen minutes early."

"Who told you that? I thought you'd never get here. You think it's easy to be rolled into shul and have everyone look at the *poor old lady*? Uch!"

"Are you saying you'd like me here earlier? I can do that."

"Not *so* much earlier. No. Not all that much. And disturb my morning?"

Laura considers turning around and walking out. That would give her such instant pleasure! But she needs the money. And Mrs. Kahn's regular home aide has gone shopping, and suppose Mrs. Kahn were to be left for hours on her own. And, then, Laura sees, in mind's eye, Binnie. So be cool. Think of her as slightly senile.

But the fact is, she seems anything but senile. Maybe a little crazy, but sharp. Okay, then. Think of her as crazy. Funny old grump. Not even that old. Bone-skinny but with hips outsized, stuffing the seat of the wheelchair. And a belly that seems outsized on a skinny woman, as if she were pregnant. Laura doesn't want to look closely.

Who knows what a stroke can do? Mrs. Kahn sounds a little drunk. She's not drunk—it's just the stroke. *Poor old lady*. But Laura senses that if she capitulates, poor old lady or not, and lets Mrs. Kahn cow her, she'll always be under her thumb, swallowing one nasty comment after the other until, finally, she explodes and quits. So in the gentlest voice she can muster, she says, "Mrs. Kahn, let me put it this way. Please listen to me. Maybe you can get away with spewing complaints onto your family . . ."

"What are you saying to me? *What* are you saying?"

"You heard me perfectly. Has your stroke affected your hearing?"

"What family? Family! Nobody comes to see me."

"I wonder why. Hmm. Let's get this straight. I don't lie. I tell the truth. And here's the truth. You treat me with respect, I'll treat you with respect. A deal?"

Silence. Well, Laura isn't going to say another thing. She isn't going to be sucked into a boring script. She knows all about those scripts from life in her own family. She knows better than to play a role. And the woman is in pain, Mrs. Kahn. She can stand and walk with a cane; holding onto chairs or the wall or a walker; she can get herself to the bathroom or even, slowly, into the kitchen to take yogurt from the fridge, but that's about it. Laura wants to give her the benefit of the doubt. Who knows what pain and incapacity can do to a person? And her husband dead. Who knows? Still, she won't be railroaded into submission. And she won't pretend.

She looks around the kitchen at the old fridge, the old cabinets. Someone's kept everything clean and neat. It's like an art installation: a 1950s kitchen, pale turquoise cabinets, white counters. The home aide keeps things nice.

Finally Mrs. Kahn speaks. "Well." She looks Laura over. "At least you're prettier than my last one. Look at that Irish red hair of yours. My driver. Pusher. Helper. Miss What's-her-name Helper had stringy hair and pimples. She wasn't even American. She spoke—God knows—I don't know what she spoke. I could hardly understand her." She peers at Laura. "And my home aide, this Janice creature, she has nothing to say to me. I might as well have a robot." She looks Laura over. "I do like your reddish hair. Laura O'Malley. You're one very pretty *shikse*."

Laura ignores this. "Will you need a sweater?"

"You've got such pretty golden hair and I must say, a peaches-and-cream complexion. Did you ever hear of Deanna Durbin? No, I'm sure not, I'm sure not."

"Her complexion?" Laura laughs. "Who cares! It's her voice I wish I had. Hollywood made her into a sweetie pie, but have you heard her sing 'Nessa Dorma' from *Turandot?*" She laughs. "Did you ever *hear* of Puccini's *Turandot?* No," she parodies, "I'm sure not, I'm sure not."

"Well, aren't you spiteful! You *are* being paid, my dear."

"Mrs. Kahn—they can't pay me enough to take abuse from you. Or to smooth over what you say. Now. You want to go to synagogue? I thought you didn't want to be late."

"Late doesn't matter all that much. It's not like church. You go to church? When I get there, I get there. You're a bit feisty, aren't you?"

"And you're a bit rude, aren't you? I told you—I'm willing to drop my act if you will please drop yours. Now, can I get you a sweater?"

"You—you're not dressed for synagogue. You're dressed like—a hippie."

Well, in a way Laura can see what she means. She's wearing tight jeans and a pretty flowered blouse showing cleavage and over one breast the small tattoo of a butterfly. She'd seen her role as a worker, not a participant. "You'd like me to dress up? I will next time."

"I'll tell you what. My daughter has put on pounds over the years. She's not fat—but she's thick. Well. She's going on fifty-five. She left some lovely, simple, nice clothes here when she was a young mother, clothes that don't fit her anymore. They're lovely, and they'll fit you. Much nicer than that skimpy blouse you're wearing. You'll do me a favor if you try something on."

Again Laura has a choice—she can tell the old lady *I dress as I dress*. Or thank her and push the wheelchair, as Mrs. Kahn helps with one hand, to roll to the guest room. Mrs. Kahn points to a pretty flowered silk blouse hanging in the closet—"You like that one, Miss Rude?" And a hand-embroidered soft wool jacket—"A bit overkill with the jeans but not impossible. I know that these days everyone wears jeans. And you, you have some figure! My goodness."

"Very nice things. Beautiful. Really? Thank you. Doesn't your daughter have children?"

"Boys. Young men. You can change right here. I'll wait outside." She rolls away, stops at the door. "Tell me. You'll sit by me at services?"

"Of course I'll sit by you."

"I must warn you. You can expect to be bored to

death in synagogue."

Laura changes and stares at herself in the mirror over the dresser. It's as if she's become somebody else. She'd never have bought these clothes—never have been able to afford them. Look at the labels! They don't go with this simple house. But she likes this romantic person she's become. She collects her hair in her hands and twisting it into a kind of chignon, she gives herself a seductive glance over her shoulder. *Well, look at me!* What would her mother say?

"Well, don't you look nice!" Mrs. Kahn, rolling in, inspects her. "Not at all like my daughter I must say. You have, as they used to say, rather a noble carriage. But now it's time."

Laura rolls the wheelchair down the ramp to the driveway.

"My children want me to have an electric wheelchair. I absolutely refuse," she says. "They're ugly machines. And dangerous."

Yet Mrs. Kahn's van has a wheelchair-accessible power lift to raise the chair to the floor of the van. This is electric, too, Laura notes.

Mrs. Kahn points. "Have you used one of those? You have to be very careful."

"I've been taught by my supervisor." Laura locks the chair into place and straps Mrs. Kahn to the chair. "You have a very nice house," she says, trying to erase and start over.

"You won't drive too fast, will you? That's all I need — an accident."

"We'll go as slow as you want. So . . . how long have you lived in your house?"

"Since I was a young wife. Almost sixty years ago. My husband came to teach. You, what's-your-name — Laura? You probably can't believe I was ever a young wife."

"Or that I'll ever be your age? I know what you mean. But I *do* believe it. I mean I *get* it, I feel it, the way time passes. I had a grandmother I loved dearly, Mrs. Kahn."

"She wasn't like me, I'll wager."

"No, that's a fact."

Services have begun when they get to synagogue. Mrs. Kahn tilts back her head and whispers, "A stroll, miss. A *stroll*, gracious, decorous. I want you to think of me — now you listen — as a duchess being carried down the aisle in a sedan chair."

"You got it, Duchess."

A middle-aged man with a grand smile comes up the aisle to help; he removes a chair from the end of a row so Laura can replace it with the wheelchair, asks, "How are you, Doris?"

"Oh, Sam," she says, "how should I be?"

"I'm Sam Schulman," he says to Laura.

"Laura O'Malley."

"Sam is the *gabbai*. He takes charge during Torah service."

"Would you like an *aliyah*?" Sam asks Mrs. Kahn.

"Laura can stand at the Torah in your place, Doris."

"No she certainly cannot. My goodness. She's not even Jewish."

"I'm half Jewish," Laura says. "My mother is Jewish."

"Half!" Mrs. Kahn snorts.

"There. You see?" Sam says, laughing. "If you like, the Jewish half of Laura can make the blessing. Kidding, dear. Kidding. Or you can sit where you are, and I can make the blessing for you, Doris. *With* you. Okay?"

"No thank you, Sam. But I appreciate."

Sam kisses her cheek and goes back to the bima.

"Bored to absolute *death*," the duchess whispers with strange delight. "You'll see."

And that first Saturday morning Laura *is* bored. And weighed down, holding for Mrs. Kahn the large-print edition of the prayer book. A heavy tome, the weight of two ordinary hardcover prayer books. And what does any of it mean? The Hebrew — the alphabet is just a blur of squiggles to her; the transliteration — meaningless sounds. And the translations? Lofty abstractions of praise. How can anyone believe a word? Praise, praise; gratitude, gratitude. She thinks of prayer as asking some God beyond this world — a God impossible to believe real — for help, and she turns to Mrs. Kahn. "Aren't there supposed to be any, you know, real *prayers*? Like making requests of God?"

The Duchess, amused, whispers in her slightly drunken mumble, "Not on Shabbat, my dear, no asking on Shabbat. You see, it's supposed to be *so* beautiful, Shabbos, Shabbat, that we're supposed to just be grateful. We're given a second soul, a Shabbat soul. We aren't supposed to *want* to make changes in the world. Now, isn't that dumb! What a joke. I'm supposed to be grateful for what? — my stroke? How delightful." She leans over and whispers, "My husband Larry and I fought like cats and dogs about this."

But still she wants to be at synagogue.

The one streak of energy, of passion, for Laura is the music. At times the melodies aren't especially Jewish. Ordinary Western music. But then there's a strange brew that sounds ancient, modal, dark, and brings tears to her eyes, whatever the words mean. Later, because Laura is a singer, the music plays over and over in her head.

"Will you please hold the book a little higher?" Mrs. Kahn sighs. "The doctor doesn't want me to sit with my neck bent down."

"Of course. Okay if I rest my elbow on the arm of the chair?"

Mrs. Kahn shrugs. She narrows her eyes, peers. "I see tears. Do I see tears?"

"It's the music," Laura whispers.

"Pretty peculiar for a *shikse*, wouldn't you say?"

She doesn't answer. And she doesn't answer. Oh, boy! She could say, *My mother was born a Rosen, I'm not exactly a shikse.* She could say, *Oh, you nut case, why do you want to make me into a spiteful brat?* She says nothing. The

Torah scroll, covered in velvet, is removed from the ark, and those who can stand, stand as it makes its way down the aisle. They kiss the fringes of their tallis or the corner of their prayer book or simply their fingers, and touch the kiss to the scroll in its robe and pointed silver caps. Mrs. Kahn reaches with her good arm, and Sam Schulman lowers the scroll to let her touch it without straining.

Laura holds her breath the moment when someone lifts the Torah scroll, unrolling it a little to show the text to the congregation. It's like opera! She resists being moved; she's moved. With that gesture of upholding the scroll literal truth seems as irrelevant as it seems in opera. The whole story, Moses and the Torah in the desert, it all becomes, for the moment, real.

At the end of the service, Mrs. Kahn doesn't want to join the congregation for lunch. "Just take me home. Who wants to be packed into a damned social hall? They'll make a fuss over me because I was one of the founders of the community. One of the last of my generation."

As she pushes the wheelchair up the aisle, Laura feels a tap on her shoulder. It's Sam Schulman. "Thank you for bringing Doris. We've missed her lately. This will be a regular thing? You'll be driving her?"

Laura steps back out of hearing. "If I can bear it," Laura says in a whisper. "Is she always like this?"

"It was different when her husband was alive. Larry died about five years ago. She used to be a social worker. And then she had her stroke."

"Well?" says Mrs. Kahn. "Are you just going to chatter and leave me sitting here?"

"Sorry," Laura says. "Sorry."

Spring in Boston. In a small, soundproof music room Laura is rehearsing, for performance by orchestra and chorus at B.U., the second and third sections of Handel's *Messiah,* practicing the beautiful soprano solo, "I know that my Redeemer liveth." Saturday mornings she takes Mrs. Kahn to services. Laura's good with languages. At times, when she should be practicing piano or voice or studying counterpoint or writing an essay on Virginia Woolf, she sneaks in an hour's study of Hebrew — first the alphabet, then prayer phrases she hears again and again. She listens to the prayers online, replays and sings along until she has them.

Partly, it's out of spite she studies. Well, not exactly spite — but to surprise Mrs. Kahn. Strange that she's become important enough to Laura to care to surprise her. On the fourth Saturday morning, on the drive to synagogue, Laura chants for Mrs. Kahn the Shema — "*Shema Y'israel, Adonoy Eloheynu, Adonoy Echad.*"

"Why, you do have a marvelous voice," says Mrs. Kahn. "Would you like to know what those strange syllables mean?"

"I know what they mean," says Laura, as if she were a little girl excited to show off for her Binnie. "'Hear O Israel, the Lord our God, the Lord is one.'"

"My goodness. My goodness."

Now comes Laura's real surprise. She goes on to chant the *next* passage, forty-one words in music that's been chanted for a millennium. More! No harder than learning an aria in Italian. And she translates, "And you shall love Adonoy, your God . . ."

"My goodness!"

Easy to parrot words and music. It's a trick—what opera singers who don't know German or Italian learn to do. She even knows what the words mean. But hasn't taken them inside.

Laura has taken out from the University library a book about Passover, almost upon them. She asks, "Doris?" — Now it's more often 'Doris' than 'Mrs. Kahn'— "Your son and your daughter, will they be coming to you for Passover? Or will you be with friends for a Seder?" She knows neither is likely; she thinks that's very sad. Why pick at old scabs? What's the good?

"Neither, my dear. I won't be needing you to drive me. There was a time Larry led a Seder for a dozen people. And I—I hunted through the house for leavened food—for *chametz*. I brought out my Passover plates and boiled silverware. You don't have to tell me about Passover. No longer. I have Janice buy a box of matzos. That's all it comes down to.

"But," she continues, "just after Passover is my husband's *yahrzeit*, and for that, I *will* need you—in the middle of the week. Do you think you could take me very early one morning?"

"*Yahrzeit*? What's that? It's German, right? —*year-time*. Meaning what, Mrs. Kahn?"

"A *yahrzeit*? The day someone in your family died. We say Kaddish. We remember."

They're more comfortable together now. Laura doesn't need to be constantly vigilant against attack. She's been given, sweater by sweater, skirt by skirt, a wardrobe of beautiful clothes. Cashmere. Silk blouses. When she wears something from this wardrobe, out of the corner of her eye she sees Mrs. Kahn staring at her and almost smiling. No, it's not exactly a smile — it's better and odder — a loving stare not aware of itself. Loving! Can you imagine? Laura still remembers the bulldog face she saw that first day. Now she finds herself offered the role of Model Daughter, Replacement Daughter; and she accepts it, fingers crossed, knowing it's conditional, temporary.

They've begun to have a sweet time, she and Mrs. Kahn, sitting over tea each week, a couple of gracious ladies, when they return from synagogue. Janice, Doris' regular home health aide, boils water for them and goes back to the television. Sometimes, after tea, Laura helps Doris into her bed, and, while it's not her role — it's Janice's — she rubs Doris' feet and legs with oil. Her feet are so dry and cold, her hands so cold. Her skin is etched, a topographical map. Laura rubs with oil and sings — sings quietly — songs from Rodgers and Hammerstein musicals.

"I do love the way you sing," Mrs. Kahn says, and lies on the bed, eyes shut.

One day, when Doris is particularly alert and the day is clear and warm, Laura makes a suggestion. "You'll probably grouch at me or laugh, Doris —"

"Would I ever do such a thing?"

"Never! Foolish me. But listen. Suppose I ride you around the neighborhood in the wheelchair. You think? The sidewalk's in good shape, and it's such a nice day. Sunny, no snow or ice."

"The wheels will get filthy."

"I'll wash the wheels when we get back. You'll enjoy it."

"I see. As if the wheelchair were a stroller and I — well, I were three years old?"

"Never mind. Just never mind then. You are *something*, Mrs. Kahn!"

"No, no, it's a very sweet idea. Are you really up to the task? We're heavy."

"The wheelchair, a little. You, I wish were heavier. You're so light. Let's try. You don't help push. You keep your fingers clean. I'll push."

"Do you know? I haven't been out since the stroke — except by car. Or ambulance."

And yet, when she bundles up Mrs. Kahn and they walk past one house, two, three, it turns out she knows stories of each family. A woman two doors down, gray hair tied up in a kerchief, is on her knees in her garden, weeding and loosening soil for spring. Doris points with her chin: "This one, this Mrs. Dalton, old lady now, she used to live across the street—in that house over there. Then she began a romance with the man from this house. This was—I don't know—forty years ago. She went from a banker to a biologist. From her old garden to her new one. Both the men are dead and gone now." Doris calls out, "Hello, Molly. Mrs. Dalton!"

"Oh, hello. It's been such a long time. Lovely to see you."

"And you! And you," Doris says, waving and smiling. Then, when they pass the house, Doris whispers to Laura—"I know, I'm a terrible gossip. And see—" she points—"that next house? Their wild little boy crashed his sled into a tree, Godforbid. In a coma for months. We all made meals for the family. But he came out of it, thank God. Now he's a pediatrician."

A valuable walk. Doris, too, may be coming out of a coma.

Laura, surrogate daughter, wonders about Mrs. Kahn's own daughter. "Have you told Harriet about me?"

"Yes, yes, of course."

"Have you told her you've been giving away her beautiful clothes?"

"Please, my dear. That is not your concern." Doris gets back on her high horse. But then she considers and holds the forefinger of her usable hand in the air as she makes a point. "My daughter doesn't call me. My daughter doesn't visit. She doesn't like me, Harriet, my daughter. It's very peculiar."

Not so peculiar to Laura, who knows what Doris Kahn can be like. She wishes she could help. But she knows better. She could never help her parents when she was growing up. She learned to play a role, keeping her growing self safe from them.

Suppose she calls Harriet. Suppose she finds her email address and writes. But without Mrs. Kahn's approval? That would be a disaster.

One Saturday, when Laura is fixing tea for them, she hears a patch of conversation from the bedroom: it's Mrs. Kahn and her daughter. Doris Kahn has put the phone on speaker so she can hear better. Laura listens to the war between mother and daughter.

"Harriet, my dear? *This . . . is a call . . . from the cemetery.*" Mrs. Kahn's voice is mournful, a rhythmic chant more than ordinary speech. Is it a joke? No, no joke.

"You mean, Mother," sighs the distant voice—and Laura can feel the exasperation all the way from Denver— "you mean you're alone and soon you'll be in the cemetery and I don't care. I never call—you mean that as far as I'm concerned, you might as well be dead? Oh, Mother. Please. That's not funny. Not amusing. And not true. Really tiresome. I call you every single week. Which is more than I can say for my brother."

"Joel! That's a whole other story. I called because your

father's yahrzeit is this Tuesday. I wanted you to know. In case you care."

"That must be by the Hebrew calendar. For the rest of us it's a week from Friday."

Laura has stopped preparing tea. She tries to catch the conversation.

The phone, old fashioned, heavy — the receiver slams down. When Laura brings in the tea, as she stirs in the honey she says, says casually, "Your daughter?"

"Daughter!"

Laura leans forward. "Doris, can I tell you something, please? I know from my own family. You're making yourself a victim. Oh, Mrs. Kahn dear, I know I have no right. You can tell me to shut up. But I know from my own family. You're pushing her away from you."

"I don't know what you're talking about."

"Oh, you do. You're very smart."

"Thank you for that. Never mind. Tell me, my dear. Can you take me to synagogue very early in the morning next Tuesday? Can you be here at seven? I've called Sam Schulman. He'll make sure there's a full minyan."

"Sure. I'll be here — before I go to class. Oh, Mrs. Kahn. Doris. Families," Laura says, "families. They're so crazy, aren't they? They're so, so sick. I'll never live that way. I refuse to live that way. My mother and father hardly speak to one another. It's always been like that. They're each other's hell, Mrs. Kahn."

"You see!"

"See? See what? Oh, Doris, I'm really sorry—for you and your daughter. Tell me. Would you like me to talk to Harriet?"

"Of course not! What can a child like you do?" She heaves a great breath. "But thank you, I do thank you, really, for wanting to help." Then, suddenly, "Laura! Do *not* put your cup down on the table!"

It's at this moment that Laura really feels it. She doesn't know why it hits her this way—the real suffering that Mrs. Kahn lives with. Not drama-queen self-pity, so false, even comic, but the real suffering of living one-sided, all the time in physical pain, all the time barely able to make herself a cup of tea. Audio books her companions, her husband gone, her son in Los Angeles, her daughter in Denver. She feels what it's like, underneath the drama, to be Doris Kahn.

Later, when Janice is taking Doris' blood pressure, Laura takes Doris' black address book from an end table and finds Harriet's number, Joel's number—just in case she ever needs them. She fingers them as contacts into her own phone. She feels a little like a thief; what she's stolen is inclusion in the family.

At the synagogue on a Tuesday morning she wheels Doris past the large sanctuary to a small sanctuary with lots of spring light from clearstory windows, a wooden podium, a semicircle of chairs, an ark closed off with a blue velvet curtain—an ark holding, she guesses, a Torah scroll. And here's that nice Sam Schulman in his full-body tallis — like a white Superman cape with blue trim and long fringes hanging down at the corners.

Mr. Schulman turns his head from the ark, smiles, stops chanting long enough to say, "We'll have our ten, don't worry, don't worry" — for now there are, including Mrs. Kahn and Laura, just eight. And Laura guesses they won't count an O'Malley in the minyan.

He goes back to his praying in a murmur. Laura takes a prayer book for Mrs. Kahn; a young mother, her baby in a sling, leans over and whispers, "The psalm on page 22."

Now three more congregants come in, then another. There's a full minyan. Plus Laura. Doris sighs and says, loud enough to be heard through the room, "Well. *Fi*nally."

Laura, reaching over, squeezes her hand. "Shh."

Doris stays seated while praying the *Amidah* — the standing prayer. But when it's time for the *Mourners' Kaddish*, she taps Laura for assistance and struggles to her feet. Before the ark, Sam, who's turned to the minyan, says, "You don't have to stand, Doris." And she snaps back, "I *know* that." Still, she stands. Holding the handles of the wheelchair, she reads in her slurred voice the Aramaic text — it's spoken, not sung — held up for her by Laura. But she doesn't need the text.

Laura does. She reads the English and sees it has nothing to do with death, with loss. It's a glorification of God, while acknowledging that no praise of God is sufficient or can come close to expressing God's holiness. And

Laura, though sure she doesn't believe in a "God," finds herself moved, tears swelling in her eyes. So "truth" isn't the point. Belief isn't the point. The prayer asks for peace. And, mysteriously, the poetry, spoken, not sung, with its repetitions of rhythm, repetitions of rhyme, *enacts* peace, brings it into being, brings peace even to Laura, standing beside Mrs. Kahn, helping to support her. A different kind of truth. A strange peace, built on surrender, though surrender is the opposite of the way Laura has lived her life.

This is the moment. Something happens to Laura. She can't say what. It's as if she just walked through the doors of a conservatory turned into tropical rain forest. Walking out of the small sanctuary, pushing the wheelchair, she finds her breath hot, as if the unwept tears were in her chest, in her mouth. Oh, she's able to ask Doris about her husband and take in what Doris says. But beneath the conversation a change is taking place in her.

Doris is telling her about Larry. He taught Legal Studies at Tufts. He retired and two years later was dead of a massive heart attack. "We always knew he had to be careful about his heart. We were the same age; I wanted to go before him. I still want to go. You call this a life?"

Laura takes a long breath. "Doris? What about the prayer you just said?"

"What about it?"

"Don't you believe it?"

"Don't make me laugh. My dear, how can you speak

at your age? The Kaddish? — it's for *me*, for *my* comfort."

"Only for you?"

"You are a very odd girl. Tell me. Do you have friends your own age?"

Laura laughs. "Actually? No. Not many. Fellow musicians. I'm sorry I spoke," Laura says. "It's not my business." She says nothing more. She pushes the wheelchair to the van.

Now, three months in, if they disagree, they say so. It's all right. No longer quarrelsome, each permits the other to disagree. "What's wrong with a good argument?" Doris asks. Laura is better able to speak freely with Doris than with her own parents. In the absence of Doris' Harriet, she, Laura, has become child or grandchild.

Her parents live in Western Mass, in Pittsfield, near the New York border. "This coming Saturday," she tells Doris, "I have to go home to see them. It's my mother's birthday. Want me to find someone to take my place for the day?"

Doris, sitting over tea, shrugs. "No, no. I can miss a week at synagogue." She holds up her teacup, delicate china, as if it were a glass of champagne. She toasts. "You, my dear, you've been very reliable, and very, very kind, very sweet. I so look forward to seeing you every week."

Laura's face grows hot. "It's meant a lot to me. You've meant lot to me." They look into each other's eyes — just for a moment they make a connection like deep friends. Who would have imagined?

The next Saturday Laura calls her from the road. "Everything is coming into bloom, Doris. I'll take pictures to show you, but they won't show much. How are you feeling?"

"Tired this morning. Very. Just as well I didn't go to services."

"I'll call you when I'm driving back tomorrow. Okay?"

Being home is always hard for Laura. It's not lack of love. Separately, there's kindness between her and each of her parents. But there's a war on between her mother and her father. Doors slam. Voices hiss. She wants to protect them from one another. It's hard. She's supposed to be the peacemaker, to listen, to calm, to soothe, to smooth over. They quarrel about the jam, about how dark the toast should be. About bills, about real and imagined affronts. She may be the perfect daughter with Mrs. Kahn; at her parents' house she mostly keeps her head down when the bullets start to fly. Each parent wants her agreement that what he or she sees is what's real. The truth. What's real, what's true, is mutual contempt. She'll be glad to be back in Boston.

Sunday. She pulls over just past the Turnpike ticket booth and calls Doris. It's raining hard. With the wiper blades turned off, the car is clouded by water; she can barely see through the glass. Doris doesn't answer. Has Janice taken her out for a walk? What — in the rain? Or has

Janice or the other home aide, a young woman who sometimes spells Janice, taken her shopping? Surely she isn't being driven to a doctor's appointment, not on a Sunday. She tells herself she's being foolish. It's her parents she's really worrying about. And for them she can't do a thing.

A half hour later she pulls into a service area and calls again. No answer. Now she's worried, imagines Janice gone, Doris fallen to the floor. Should she call the agency that pays her? Instead, she scrolls her contacts, calls Harriet Mellon, and the phone is answered at once. "Harriet? I'm Laura O'Malley. I take care of your mother sometimes. I'm just a little worried about her, your mother doesn't answer her phone. I'm on the road. I'll stop in when I get back. I'm sure she's okay, I'm just a little worried."

And Harriet says: "She's not okay. I'm at the airport. I can't talk. We're boarding. My mother has had a heart attack. She's at Mass General. I'm flying in."

Doris' children have both gone home. Laura drives by on a spring evening after her classes. The house is closed up; a contractor will prepare it for sale. The van is gone. She turns off the engine and stares at the house, imagining that it's 1970, and a young faculty member and his wife are moving in with a baby. That baby who would become Joel.

Harriet was with her mother in the hospital when the aneurism burst. Joel flew in from Seattle. Harriet's husband and sons couldn't come, Joel's wife didn't come.

After the little service and burial — just a few old people — they stayed in the house a night and two days. The rabbi made an announcement that there would be a "shiva minyan," and he led an evening service; friends, congregants who knew her, came. The rabbi covered mirrors with cloths; it annoyed Harriet and Joel, but they let him pretend they were sitting shiva.

Laura came. Some visitors, who'd known the children growing up, nudged them to tell stories about their mother. Harriet put pictures on the tables but didn't say much. No one spoke about Doris' late anger, her sense of injustice. Now it was Harriet who was angry. Angry at what? Bitter. Unsatisfied. Out of the corner of her eye Laura saw Harriet's eyes rimmed with tears. But her face was tight, and no tears came.

Laura remembered the bulldog woman she first saw in this house. Laura sees it in Harriet, Doris' look that first day they met, though softened by sadness.

After the funeral, after evening service, Joel and Harriet tagged pictures and books, lamps, furniture for shipping or giving away, and they went through the house with a pad making notes for the contractor. They paid Laura, insisted on paying her, to help them clear the house. She boxed, to give away, paraphernalia of a stroke patient; dumped into a contractor's bag as garbage, medicines and stained linen; rolled the wheelchair into the garage and tagged it as a contribution to the Senior Center. Joel flew back to Seattle to work; Harriet and Laura stayed on an extra day.

On the instructions of the contractor, Harriet and Laura cleared rooms, stuffing the living room with chairs, lamps, tables. They stopped for tea — it's the last time Laura would ever see the pretty flowered china, which then they washed, protected with bubble wrap and boxed for shipping.

"I'm sure my mother wasn't easy these past months," Harriet says. "But you know — she could be wonderful — funny, tender. In the old days. Really until my dad died and then the stroke. You got the worst of it. Joel and I are so grateful to you, your kindness, what you did for her."

"I really didn't get the worst."

Laura turns over and over in her mind fragments of that awful phone conversation she overheard. *You* got the worst: this she doesn't say. Both of you. It's especially in family, Laura says to herself, that people are so awful to one another. But what good to bring that up? She says, "We got past her anger. I grew to love her."

Harriet closes her eyes and heaves a breath, taking this in.

She'll never see Harriet again. She so much wants to soothe her, to make things all right between Harriet and her mother. To make peace. Retroactively. Forever. How can that be? And then — oh, then she gets it, gets how to do that. *Of course.*

"Over and over," Laura says, "she told me, especially these last couple of months, how much she loved you. Maybe she couldn't say it to you, but you can't imagine how often she told me. She said you fought and fought but deep down you both knew how you loved each other."

"She said that? Oh, she was just being sentimental. It wasn't true. She loved me?"

"Absolutely true. Oh, she was bitter at times — losing your dad, and then the stroke — she could barely walk, her speech so damaged. But her big secret was loving you. That's what kept her going, made her happy when she was happy. You got the worst of it — she wouldn't tell you. I wanted her to say it to you, but you know how stubborn she could be. Me, she could tell: she loved you both, you and Joel — but especially you. She was so proud of you. I nagged her to tell you — at least over the phone. She said, 'Oh, Harriet knows, Harriet knows.'"

Harriet's face opens. The bulldog look dissolves. Harriet walks into the living room, she sits down and weeps. She rocks back and forth. She weeps.

Laura has lied, but in a deeper sense, hasn't she told the truth? Would Doris have been so bitter if she hadn't loved Harriet? It's because she cared so much that she was so demanding. And Harriet wouldn't hurt so much if she didn't love her mother.

Of course they loved each other.

And now, she thinks, as she sits in her car looking at the house this spring night, what about my own family? *Haven't I exaggerated the importance of literal truth? Look at the power of fiction.* Suppose she speaks to her mother when her father's not around — to her father when her mother's

out. Let each know what the other has "said." Love? No,
that they wouldn't believe. But respect? Admiration?
Who knows what might come of it?

It's early May, Tuesday morning at the synagogue.
Daffodils and tulips line the flagstone sidewalk to B'nai
Shalom. Laura O'Malley is here on her own this time, part
of the minyan. She's here mostly to say Mourners' Kaddish.
She knows that Doris' son Joel won't say Kaddish, Harriet
won't say Kaddish. Who else is there? Sam Schulman put
his arm around her shoulder at the burial when she wept.
Laura asked him: *I'm not family; can I say Kaddish?*
   "Of course. She'd be grateful."
   "I'll say it on Tuesday mornings. And on Shabbat
when I can."
   "Lovely!"
So this sunny Tuesday morning, golden light broad-
cast aslant through clearstory windows onto the maple
flooring and wall panels, suffusing, it seems, the air,
Laura sits down close to Sam, who's leading the service.
He looks like a giant bird, the tallis like wings. His throaty
baritone rough but pleasant, he murmurs the Hebrew
much faster than she can read, so she floats on his chanting, takes a ride, feels a connection with him and with the
young mother with baby in sling, who sits beside her, and
an old man, rocking and murmuring. When it comes time,
Sam turns to look at her and nods. "I'll say it with you,"
he tells her. A couple of others are also reciting Mourners'

Kaddish today. Sam sets a slow pace. Laura follows.

It's as if she's holding a soul in her hands. But more. She's taken into herself the chants and the prayers. While she stands there, they're the truth, the real thing. It's not that she believes she's praising some gent in the heavens. Belief, indeed, isn't the point. Standing and rocking, she finds herself entering a truth created by chants and prayers — truth engendered by the ten, eleven, twelve of them standing in the little room lit by spring morning light from the clearstory windows.

The Grandparent Option

IT'S APRIL. The snowbirds are flying back from Florida and Hawaii, and Tuesday mornings at 7:30 a few are to be seen perching again in the little sanctuary at B'nai Shalom — Children of Peace — unaffiliated synagogue in Brookline, Mass. Winters, many retired people go away, so it's hard to raise a full minyan: ten adult Jews. Without ten there are prayers that can't be said — the *Barekhu*, a *Kaddish*.

For most of the winter Gershom and Susannah Samuels visit their children and grandchildren — in California, in Arizona. Everyone's pleased to see Gershom back at the morning service. He's important to the community not just as one counted in a minyan; he's deeply, knowledgably Jewish — one of the wise older men of the larger congregation. He grew up in Brooklyn, son of a family that fled Austria just in time, leaving limbs of the family behind. The limbs died.

He's observant, though not, like his parents, Orthodox. But when he's in town, it's to Gershom — even more than to Rabbi Stein or Professor Alex Koenigsberg — they turn when a question comes up. Do you remove tefillin when you chant Hallel? What's the history of the Sabatai Zvi heresy?

He's a scholar. Retired from Judaic Studies at Boston University, he writes for Jewish newspapers and since his retirement has published the best recent book on *Zionism and the Diaspora.* Every Friday, Gershom and the rabbi and Sam Schulman and a professor from Tufts, Alex Koenigsberg, do a page of Talmud in the rabbi's office. Yet he's a mild, even humble man. Long and angular, a Don Quixote by Picasso, he has a sweet smile with overtones of sadness. It's a sadness that those who meet him read as wisdom. He doesn't feel wise, certainly doesn't mean to come off as wise. It's simply: to be in this world, how can you be not sad?

Tuesday. Sam Schulman, leading the morning service, without, as yet, a full minyan, turns from the ark to greet Gershom. "You're back! Welcome. Welcome." And Kate Schiff says, "Shalom, Gershom." They've noticed a small boy at his side, how old?—five? six?—holding on like a shadow to his leg. Sam wants to run his fingers through the child's hair—but knows better, refrains. Just smiles. "And who's this guy?" he asks.

"This guy? This is my grandson, Kyle."

This winter vacation began, for Gershom and Susannah, undramatic, pleasant. They visited their son David, and Cindy, and their two girls in Seattle. If there was unease, urgency, it was merely in trying to make up, in so little time, for being grandparents a continent away. Not easy keeping a relationship going by visits twice a year.

Then the more problematic visit — to their daughter Eve in San Diego.

Eve is alone now with their grandson, her son Kyle — she's been alone for six months — and laughs that she's "now a full-fledged single mom." Eve always tries to be upbeat. So at the airport she tells them, Oh! She's doing so well. "My career! There's so much to tell but first let's get you settled."

Everything seems lovely, but something's wrong: Eve seems uneasy. Gershom knows right away and exchanges a glimpse with Susannah. She nods. On the way home — a house north of San Diego, they pick up Kyle at school, a private school. Eve pulls her Lexus into line, and when the kids burst from the front door, she hops out of the car to kiss Kyle, leads him to the back seat, to his grandmother's lap a moment; then plunks him onto his booster seat and he straps himself in.

Susanna puts her arm around him and asks, "May Grandma kiss you? Oh, I've missed you so much," she says, and doesn't wait for an answer. Eve, catching a glimpse in the rear-view mirror says, "Mom! What are you crying about? Kyle, honey — do you have one silly grandma?"

Such a beautiful child, Gershom thinks. Tall and lean — hair golden like his absent father's.

They drive north out of San Diego towards La Jolla. Sunshine, sunshine, sunshine. Houses with perfect lawns and pools. A beautiful, broad, tree-lined road, no potholes from freezing and melting. Why in heaven's name, he wonders, do they continue to live in the Northeast? Oh, Gershom knows why. Friends, community, volunteer work. And then there's simple inertia. But every time he comes here he wonders: are they crazy living where they don't see the grandchildren and where one day it's freezing rain, the next snow, then for a change an ice storm?

Sitting up front, Gershom looking steadily at his beautiful daughter, sees that Eve herself is nearly in tears. Are her eyes wet? Her eye liner is blurred and the rims of her eyes are red. He doesn't ask.

She asks. "What?"

He shrugs. "You, honey. You. Are you really doing okay?"

"Sure. Sure, Dad. A good bit of okay. Wait. I'll tell you when we're home."

She's always been their drama-child. At thirty-six, no difference. He can imagine how she reacted to Dan when she felt frustrated. Sure. Dan must have gone totally silent, retreated totally into himself and she, she would have beaten at the high walls to get at him. He imagines nights of broken plates, high-pitched demands, and a wall of silence. Well—when they split up, Dan called them to explain and said as much. A nice enough man. A dull man. Successful, steady. Not much of a father. But she chose him eyes open. A heartache for Gershom and Susannah because it's a heartache for Eve.

Eve says nothing till they've unpacked and given gifts to Kyle and Eve. Kyle wanders off to play a video game on the big-screen TV. The noise of laser whines and machine gun chatter makes Gershom wince. Eve, Susannah, Gershom sit in the breakfast nook surrounded by tall windows and French doors. "Well, the big news," Eve says, almost whispers, "is my New Position. Capital N, capital P, omigod."

Before she tells them about it, she dances her hands through the air as if she were conducting an orchestra. "Look, just look at this house. Lovely, right? All the latest, etcetera, right? Granite counter tops, a basement for exercise machines, plenty of space for a small regiment. But what are we doing here, just the two of us? And I hardly know anyone. We have to get in the car and drive to San Diego to see a friend or find anything happening. We should be in a city. We *should*. So, folks, I started putting out feelers, and a headhunter came after me. Looks like I'm going to accept the position of marketing manager for a European firm, a French firm, *Vive,* a line of nutrients and specialty foods — cheeses, sauces, herbs — and if it works out, very soon I'll be named Vice-President in charge of marketing."

"Why, how wonderful," her mother says. And Gershom can hear Susannah's quiet sigh — she'd been waiting, as he had, for something awful. "Why, that's marvelous," she says. "Eve, darling. Why didn't you tell us right away?"

"Well," Eve says, "the thing is, parents, I'll be in New York."

The kettle whistles; Eve jumps up to prepare the tea.

"And?" Susannah prompts.

"We're delighted," Gershom says. "We'll see much more of you."

"The thing is, the thing is — " and now she's really whispering — "*how can I take Kyle*? I can't. There's no way. To New York? Ugh. So hard. School? You think I could get him into a decent school mid-year? Even for next fall it's too late to apply."

That she'd even consider not being with Kyle pulls heavy darkness into Gershom's body. "But oh, Eve," he says, "you can find help. And we'll come down and help."

"Oh, my God. No! I'll be traveling around the country. And back and forth to Europe. I'd have to hire a live-in nanny, and I won't have that kind of money. Anyway, it would be awful for Kyle. You see? And so I thought, well, maybe my dear brother . . . until I get settled, at least. But David absolutely refuses to have Kyle come to them in Seattle. Or Cindy refuses. You know what a selfish bitch my sister-in-law can be. Oh, my God."

"But they're both working," Susannah says. "It's as hard for them as for you."

"You always favor David."

"Not true, not true," Susannah sings.

"And as for Kyle's father — Dan's new honey-bunny won't take Kyle even if I wanted that. Actually, I'm delighted. Anyway, he told me. We talked. He offered more child support. I accepted. They want nothing to do with children."

"Then what are your options?" Gershom asks — though he knows, he knows.

"Well. It's a fabulous job, Dad."

"Sounds it. I'm proud of you. But what are your options if not a nanny?"

"I *thought*. I thought that, okay, I'd take the job — of *course* — and you and Mom could take Kyle. For awhile. Months. A year? Give him a stable home. And when I'm in the city, I can come up to Boston and be with you and Kyle on weekends. Well. *Some* weekends." She brings cups and a wooden box filled with tea. "What tea would you like?"

From the living room they hear the sound effects of the video game. Screams and explosions. Gershom and Susannah look through the box of teas, as if tea leaves could tell them something.

"You're upset," Eve says. "I really thought you'd be overjoyed."

And in a way, Gershom *is* overjoyed and knows Susannah is overjoyed. But to manage an active six-year-old boy? He's seventy-five. He creaks. Susannah is sixty-eight. And then — and this is the real heaviness for him — he's disappointed with Eve. Kyle's lost one parent; how can she let him lose another? How can she! He'd lecture her about values, but what good will moralizing do?

At once, he takes it inside *himself*: what kind of parents were they if Eve could turn out this way?

"You're going to visit your grandparents, a nice long visit," Eve says after dinner as they take a walk along a pretty suburban street with no sidewalks. The sun's gone down; it's still light out, but Eve has brought a flashlight so drivers notice them.

"With you, Mommy?" Kyle says.

"Not right away," she says. "But soon."

"How soon?"

"Soon-soon."

"Mo-m!" Two syllables, ending down a fifth.

"Honey?" Susannah says. "You *do* have to come soon. Soon as you're settled."

"Of course, of course. Don't you think I'll *want* to?" Gershom knows she feels guilty and wants to blame her parents. *They're* the ones making her feel guilty. Then: "Oh, ya gonna just love it," Eve says to Kyle. Or to her parents. Or to herself.

And now, two weeks later, we're at the Tuesday morning minyan. "So, this is your grandson?" Sam Schulman says, turning from the ark, smiling at Kyle. "Nice! Will it be a long visit?"

"We're putting him in school in Brookline. His mother has a big job—international. We're lucky to have him with us." He turns to Kyle, wraps his arm around Kyle's shoulders. "See this nice man in the big white shawl with the fringes hanging down? This is Sam Schulman. He'll lead us in morning prayers." Gershom plunks a maroon yarmulke on Kyle's head.

Sam reaches out a hand for a shake. "Kyle," he says, "you've come to a minyan that's got lots of grandparents. But most of them" — he says this for Gershom's benefit — "aren't lucky enough to bring their grandchildren. Welcome!"

Kyle is, Gershom knows, somewhat spooked by the full-body tallis and the little black boxes strapped to arm and forehead. Eve isn't religious; Kyle's father is a totally secular Episcopalian. Now Grandpa puts on his tallis, straps on the little boxes. Gershom asks Kyle to help him strap his arm, hoping to make tallis and tefillin less strange. "We're going to pray and sing," he says to Kyle. "It's like a play, but the main character, God, has no lines."

All right, all right! He knows how little Kyle can make of that!

"It's wonderful, isn't it wonderful," Susannah asks, "at her age, a position like that?"

"Sure. She's a smart girl, a go-getter, and she's learned the language of business. Yes, I'm pleased for her."

"So what's so bad if we take care of our beautiful, exceptional grandchild for awhile?"

Kyle has been registered in the Brookline Elementary School system. Filling out the data online makes both

Gershom and Susannah feel the semi-permanence of their new condition: suddenly (at their age) to be bringing up a first grader. He'll be at the Driscoll School, walking distance from the Samuels' home. Susannah is busy this afternoon at a committee meeting for a food pantry; Gershom picks Kyle up and takes him for an ice cream; then they drive to a playground and he pushes his grandchild on the swings. "Watch me on the bars," Kyle says, climbing. "Watch! Can you climb like me?"

"I'm an old guy, Mister Kyle."

"Grandpa, please, Grandpa?"

So Gershom climbs. Twinges of arthritis, but basically he's in good shape.

"Now the slide, Grandpa!"

Lean as Gershom is, he only just fits between the wooden sides made for the hips of children. Up he climbs, down he comes, and Kyle yells in support.

"Suddenly," Gershom says, "I'm a climber of monkey bars."

Susannah, closing her laptop at the kitchen table, looks on the bright side. "You see? It'll keep us young."

"It'll make us old," he says, pretending to groan. "Or so my muscles say to me. 'Old,' they say. And especially in the morning."

"Mornings *are* hard."

"Mornings are *very* hard. My bones cry out, just when Kyle's up and crying out of his morning joy and bouncing off walls. But seriously, that's not my issue. It's Eve I'm upset about."

"Why? Because she had to choose—to sacrifice her life to her child or take a fabulous job? Really. Aren't you demanding she be the 1960 version of a mother? What an old fashioned man you are!" She's teasing but not teasing. "We're all so lucky. The Grandparent Option. Right?"

"She hasn't called for two days."

"She's getting settled. Please, Gershom!"

Kyle is digging into a box of books and toys they've brought up from the basement—once David's or Eve's. Gershom thinks, as he helps Kyle connect Lionel tracks and set down the locomotive and the cars, *I've got to show her I'm not condemning her.* Susannah's right: his basic attitude is that a mother has to think first about her child. Period. *I really am old fashioned. I should be happy about Eve. It's hard enough for her, I'm sure, being without Kyle. Why make it worse?*

He says this to himself but doesn't believe a word.

Eve's house sold within a week. She's a good organizer; the moving company has helped her sort and box. She's taken a little one-bedroom in the West Village, not far from the river. The company is paying for the move. "Grandpa? Will we go visit Mommy?" Kyle asks. "When will we?"

"Soon. We will, we will. And soon she'll visit us. She wants to see you *so* bad!"

But on Thursday, three weeks into her move, she

still can't take a weekend off. "I can understand that," Susannah says. Gershom doesn't answer. Ach! It is what it is. He has begun to know the child, to love him not as a generic grandchild but as a particular kid—soulful, a questioner—someone with curiosity, with attention. Annoying, complaining, fussy, but wonderful in a way he couldn't appreciate as a father in his thirties. In the bathtub Kyle sings to himself and makes up stories about pirates and aliens. Maybe, Gershom thinks, maybe he can help give Kyle a grounding in what it means to be a Jew, part of a Jewish community. Eve never wanted that. Maybe Kyle. On Friday night they sing "Shalom Aleichem" and chant the blessings over the candles, the wine, the challah. Susannah prepared the challah dough on Thursday night, and on Friday, after dinner, Gershom sits with Kyle and tells a story from the portion of Torah for the week. Then he teaches. One week he teaches about their challah. "This challah. Kyle, tell me: who helped make this challah and get it to the table?"

"Me and Grandma. Right, Grandpa?"

"Sure. Right. But is that all? Who else helped?"

"The people who grew the flour?"

"Good! Very good. That's the idea. And what about the truck driver who brought it to the store? And the workers who built the oven? You see? Who else?"

"The store people where we bought the flour?"

And together they started adding in the people who built the truck and the people who made the roads and the chickens and farmers who gave us the eggs and the people long ago who developed the recipe—*millions* of people—and then he got weirder: "And what about the yeast and the water and the air, and what about the laws of nature that let the dough rise—remember? And on and on." He knew that with some of this teaching he was losing Kyle. But he was on a roll. "So we praise God who brings all this together, creates all this. We call it God. But it's a mystery. There's a single unified energy that makes it all come together. It's beyond amazing. We go 'WOW! Thanks!'"

"Dear," Susannah says very quietly, "that's enough. He can't possibly understand."

"Yes I can, Grandma! I can so! We go 'Wow!'" And he runs around the kitchen. "Wow!"

"To teach a child, a grandchild, it's the most important thing," he says, raising a teaching forefinger. "The most."

"Enough. Have you asked Eve?"

"Eve? Eve's not here. Do you see her behind the sofa?"

"You can't give him a crash course in being a Jew. And without his mother's permission?"

But that's exactly what he intends to do. "Teaching is the norm," he tells Susannah. "You don't wait till a child grows up to teach him. It's to be built into his bones."

He teaches Kyle about Shabbat. "For one day a week we don't work—we just try to live, live simply and happily. We remember that God rested on the seventh day after making the world. Let me tell you the story."

On Shabbat they shut off computer and TV, he walks to synagogue. He's not consistent about avoiding work on Shabbat but, especially now that Kyle is with them, he tries.

Gershom goes to synagogue, Susannah goes for a long walk with Kyle. If Kyle stays with them, maybe in the fall they can send him to a Jewish day school. And maybe he can help wean Kyle from computer games and TV and the empty culture waiting to gobble down children. Already they've established some rules: TV or an action game for an hour a day, no more. And no killing games, period. He can exchange emails with his mom or his friends all he wants.

Kyle is, so far, polite, agreeable.

Oh, this won't last, Gershom knows. Kyle's a kid full of life energy. He'll begin asserting himself. But so far, it's been tiring—but a joy. They play games with Kyle, take him to the park, arrange play dates with classmates. Maybe it *will* keep them young.

It's a delicate balance. Gershom doesn't want to be the tough guy, the repressor, Susannah the giver. So he, too, gives. It's a wonderful time. He gets used to having cushions from the couch made into a tunnel on the living room carpet, enjoys crawling on hands and knees into a pirate cave. One afternoon Kyle kicks a soccer ball in the living room. A photo on the coffee table spins to the floor and the glass breaks.

"Sor-ry, sor-ry" Kyle says. "Sorry, Grandpa."

As a young father, Gershom would have grumped and guilt-tripped. "No problem," Gershom says now. "You're a pretty careful kid. I'll get you the broom and dust pan. Please—try hard not to get stuck by the slivers of glass."

Some nights they sit together after dinner and watch goofy old movies that Eve and David watched as kids— Kyle laughs at the Marx Brothers in *Night at the Opera*. He dons a coat of his grandfather's and a clown wig and waddles around the house honking a toy horn.

The longer Kyle stays, the more they can't bear the thought of losing him.

Eve calls, some evenings, at Kyle's bedtime, to say goodnight. And finally she says she'll be free the next weekend. Can she come up?

"Of course, of course," Susannah says, laughing. "'Can you come up!' And how's the job? Going well?"

"Quite well," Eve says. "Absolutely. And, oh yes, I may be bringing a friend."

"A friend?"

"A boyfriend. I may."

"So you'll be seeing your Mom," Gershom says, helping Kyle get into his pajama shirt. "Are you excited?"

"Uh huh. Is the man coming with Mommy?"

"What man?"

"I don't know. A man, some man. A big, tall man, he's not nice."

"She hasn't mentioned. You don't like him?"

"I hate him."

Should he say something to Kyle about hating? No. That's how the kid feels. This isn't the time for a moral lesson. Gershom knows his own tendency to moralize. There are so many better things to do to help a lovely six-year-old boy grow into a mensch.

And let's be honest: he knows himself. He's a little pleased—and is ashamed of being pleased—that Kyle rejects this new man. A little flurry of delight: it's ignoble. And bewildering.

He's dying to probe, to question. Did she meet the man in San Diego? Must have. But how did he get to New York at the same time? Nothing wrong, he tells himself— Eve meeting a man. But he's dying to know more.

They pick her up on Friday afternoon at Back Bay. Carrying the bags, walking behind her, is a very tall man. "Meet Richard Miller," she says. "My parents, Susannah and Gershom."

"Gershom," the tall man says. "Moses' son."

"Very good, very good," Gershom says.

They come, Eve and Richard, bearing gifts: fine chocolates, pesto and tapenade from Dean & Deluca, an expensive bottle of white wine. And for Kyle a compass and a DVD with a ribbon around the case—"a video of your mommy's little apartment." Smart, Gershom thinks. Encouraging Kyle to feel connected to her life. They sit in the living room and watch the video just before lighting candles for Shabbat.

"You see how small and simple my place is. But it's sweet and comfortable now that the furniture's here. A lot of it I sold or gave away. But it's magical how well my best pieces fit. I couldn't stand losing my precious things. You know? And what a fabulous location!"

A sweet little Greenwich Village apartment. But so pristine. He can't believe anyone actually lives there. No books, no mess. Maybe she worked hard to make it look perfect. Why? For them? Certainly, Kyle wouldn't care about mess.

Richard is maybe six-four, six-five, with a long, handsome head. Well groomed, slightly long hair just beginning to gray. He displays a Harris tweed sports jacket, an expensive watch, pale blue silk shirt, shiny, pointed Italian shoes. He's quiet. Maybe he's so used to standing out that he feels no need to make an effort. He listens, he smiles. If he speaks at all, it's informative, calm, thoughtful, precise. Eve's the flamboyant one, as she was when she and Dan were a couple. *Just wait a couple of years,* Gershom says to himself. Of course, Richard has power; that may make a difference.

"So find where you want to sleep," Susannah says, waving her hand around as Gershom sets the candles in their holders. Eve's too old for discretion. "Your old room?"

"Sleep with *me*, Mommy!"

"You know better than that, Kiddo. I'll tuck you in," Eve says, petting him but clearly embarrassed. Kyle pouts; but he squiggles up next to her on the couch. He's smelling her, Gershom thinks; he's taking her inside himself.

Gershom blesses the lighting of the candles, says Kiddush over the wine, blesses the bread. Eve dims her eyes and slumps in her chair to show she's bored, while Richard puts on a yarmulke and seems invested in the ceremony. Kyle wears a yarmulke but seems cut off. "Do you remember our Shabbat song?" he asks Kyle. Last week and the week before, Kyle joined right in. Not tonight.

Gershom and Susannah sing "Shalom Aleichem." Not Eve. Surprise—Richard sings along. "We sang 'Shalom Aleichem' at home when I was growing up. My father had been brought up Jewish. Seems the words are still in my mouth. Funny!" The song and blessings annoy Eve. She sighs; she slouches in her chair. Kyle, regressing from six to about four years old, slumps like his mother. Gershom sees him playing with his mother's hand, sees that he avoids ever looking at Richard—which is hard: Richard takes up so much room.

Next morning, Richard still in bed, Eve comes downstairs and fixes breakfast with her parents. She's plunked Kyle in front of the TV, and Gershom decides he won't play Shabbat policeman. It gives them, after all, a chance to talk. They toast bagels in the oven, though on Shabbat, from Friday night to Saturday night, you're supposed not to use the oven or stove.

"So," Susannah says to her daughter, "you've found yourself one handsome big guy. He works with you, right?"

"Right. I met him at a trade show. Some hunk, huh? I have to let you into a secret. He's my boss. He's the one who really worked to bring me to New York."

"Didn't you say it was a headhunter?" her mother asks.

"Oh, I say that so it doesn't look like just a personal connection."

Gershom says, "But it *is* a personal connection, right? Let me play Sherlock Holmes. That video. It tells me you hardly live in that apartment."

"Well, Dad, that's kind of true. Two nights a week. At most. *When* I'm in the city." They're at the kitchen table not even pretending to eat. "Frankly, Dad, I don't like it when you play tough cop with me. Truth is, I'm trying to cement our relationship. If Kyle were with me—you see?"

"I don't see. Tell me. If Kyle were with you—go on. Then what?"

"Then everything would fall apart. Actually, Richard wants nothing to do with children. Even his own by his first marriage. I know that sounds awful, but he's a sweet man otherwise. I'm hoping I can relax him about Kyle. Actually, that's kind of what we're doing here."

"And you're hoping that as he becomes completely head over heels in love with you, etcetera, I mean as you come closer, Kyle will be slightly acceptable to him. Will be bearable."

"The way you put it, Dad, makes it sound terrible."

"You know why?" Gershom leans forward and says, as if it's a secret he's revealing, "That's because it *is* terrible." Gershom doesn't like himself at this moment. He feels ugly. But. But we did something wrong if our daughter is what she is. He knows that Susannah will try to soft-soap him. *Shouldn't she build a career? Shouldn't she have a lovelife? Richard seems like a decent man.* And he does. Apparently, he just doesn't happen to want children. Meaning our beautiful Kyle. How long will a union based on romantic love last?

"Are you engaged to this man? Have you talked about marriage?"

"Dad, please. I'm not sixteen years old. Omigod! No, we haven't spoken about marriage."

Gershom's head is pounding with pain. He doesn't say, *Then he could dump you both as a lover and as an executive.* No, he can't say that. He goes off to get a couple of ibuprofen. He passes through the living room. There's Kyle on the floor, watching Saturday morning cartoons. And beside him, surprising Gershom again, Richard Miller, seeming twice as long as the boy. He makes Kyle look like a toddler. Gershom mumbles "Hi," sits down on the sofa behind them. He watches them watch cartoons. Richard's joking about something; Kyle's nodding but not laughing.

Theater! Theater going on everywhere you look. He knows that in the kitchen Eve will be complaining about her father's treatment of her, and Susannah will soothe. And the complaint will be, partly, dramatic enactment, as will the soothing. He can see that here in the living room Richard is playing a role as nice guy, trying to soften the stiffness between him and Kyle, and Kyle is making him work for it.

Theater, constantly. Players acting for each other but also for themselves as audience.

He heads offstage. To the medicine cabinet upstairs. But absent, he's as much part of the drama as when he's present. Returning through the living room, he asks Richard, "Want some bagels?"

"Aren't you going to synagogue this morning?" Richard asks.

"Not this Shabbat. It's too precious here, having our daughter with us."

Richard leans over, roughs up Kyle's hair and follows Gershom to the kitchen. Kyle stays in front of the TV. "One more minute, one more, okay?" So it's Gershom and Richard. Ten steps to the kitchen is all. Halfway, Gershom stops, puts a hand on Richard's sleeve and says, outright, "Tell me. Richard. How do you feel about children? Do you like children?"

"*Some* children. Sure. Kyle I certainly like. I like him a lot. And my own kids. But I was a sucker. I let my ex take them to Chicago. It's terrible."

"I thought so. Richard, we have smoked salmon. Can I get you some?"

Kyle comes to the table—he seems happy and unhappy. His bagel and cream cheese goes untasted. As if the bagel were a hockey puck he slaps it from one side of his plate to the other. He wants to tell about his new school, wants to sit beside his mother and just tell and tell, and she should listen and no one else should talk to her. And Gershom can see she's bored and caught between agendas. She's pretending to smile, half-listening to Kyle, while keeping her eye on Richard, looking for his attention, wanting to make sure he's comfortable, engaged. And Kyle knows this and talks more and more frenetically. Gershom predicts, seeing his daughter's discomfort, that it won't take Richard long to tire of her. He hopes that won't damage her career. And maybe, if they break up, she'll figure out how to live with Kyle, get some help, be a mother.

Will that ever happen? What he knows is this: the one who doesn't want Kyle isn't Richard. She'll blame it on Richard.

Gershom sips his coffee and smiles, mellow paterfamilias, pretending ease, knowing that while his every breath is permeated with the stink of moral judgment, he's eager to hold onto Kyle. Of course! In fact, in fact!— he can't stand the idea of being without the boy, so isn't he pleased that he can blame his daughter?

So much going on over bagels!

"More coffee?" he asks.

They take a Sabbath stroll on the gravel path circling the Chestnut Hill Reservoir by Boston College. Kyle walks up ahead with his mother, Richard between Susannah and Gershom. Gulls soar. Runners run. A light breeze makes the water tremble. Susannah says, "We're so blessed to have a spring day like this."

"It's lovely to be with you whatever the weather," Richard says. "And to have a quiet weekend with that young lady up ahead."

Oh, Richard is a charmer. Right now it's Susannah he's charming. "What a daughter you've raised," he sings. "Do you know how smart she is? How flexible, how creative. She comes into a new position and shapes it fruitfully. She's already begun to grow new markets. Let me speak frankly, Susannah, Gershom: I was uneasy bringing her to New York. But it *is* working out."

Now he stops and turns to Gershom. "At the same time I know Eve is desperate to be a good mother. She's a little afraid that she isn't meeting your expectations in that arena, Gershom. Is she right? Believe me, she couldn't love that boy any more than she does. You know, actually — it's one of the things about her that really moves me."

Gershom is impressed by his openness. And almost hopeful. But he can't resist saying, "I'm sure you're right. But at a distance, how much good does that love do Kyle?"

Richard says, "It's not easy for either of them. We're both grateful that you've been able to take care of Kyle." Richard's too smart to get in an argument. Gershom finds he admires the young man. He's shrewd. And when he talks to you he's really with you. They walk in silence.

"Love," Gershom sighs at last. "This is what I think, Richard. Feelings can't be relied on. Your life must be known by, has to be grounded in, norms of conduct—you get me?—norms of conduct that *hold* feelings within borders—that *trump* feelings. Eve gushes love, love, love over Kyle. And really feels it, feels that love. I know. Meantime, she doesn't call to say goodnight."

"She's been so busy."

Again, there's silence. Finally, Richard, not wanting to be put in this position, calls ahead, "Mind if I join you, Eve?"

"Three's a crowd," she says, her hands to her mouth like a megaphone. "Kyle and I, we're discussing heavy matters. Wait a few minutes."

Gershom is uneasy. He wishes he had a parabolic surveillance microphone he could aim up ahead and find out what Eve is saying to Kyle.

What's real? People may think they love children and yet want to be the one pampered and fussed over. Or they love one minute, are bored the next; or love in one context, not in another; feel one way when with their lover, differently when with their lover's child. Love the child but not be ready to be a full-time mother.

"All right, Monsieur Richard," Eve calls. "I think we're ready for you."

And Richard excuses himself and jogs the gravel path to join mother and son. Gershom takes Susannah's hand.

They're in pajamas, brushing their teeth when Eve knocks at their bedroom door. "Can we talk a minute?"

Susannah says, "Of course, dear. Close the door behind you."

They sit on the bed, the three of them. How long has it been since the last time Eve hung out on her parents' bed? Gershom, remembering Eve as a child, finds tears welling up. He doesn't let her see.

"You guys, you've been such a godsend. My baby seems so much bigger and stronger than when I left him. It's been what? — a month?"

Gershom keeps himself from saying, *Almost two months.*

"Maybe we ought to take Kyle to New York. To live with us."

"Didn't you say —"

"—that Richard didn't like kids? Yes, well maybe I was exaggerating."

"Maybe you didn't *want* him to like Kyle too much. Maybe you're afraid that if you were with a child full-time, it would dim your 'display' — I'm thinking of the display by some birds — male birds, but you get the point — to win a mate. And to shine. Isn't that what you've been doing?"

"God, you're so moralistic. Mother, am I so terrible? So I want to give myself to my work for awhile. And yes, yes, I want to be seen as a fabulous, independent woman — why not? And Richard and I — I know how much harder it will be for me to build something with Richard if Kyle's under foot. Richard and I both know it. But maybe I can find a grad student to help. Okay?"

Suddenly, Gershom, tears brimming, wraps his arms around Eve. He's in panic; he has no idea he's going to say this: "Listen, I'm sorry, honey, I've been the way I've been. So tough on you. Please, please don't take him. Please, leave him here with us. For awhile. A few months? A year or two? We can work it out, visit back and forth."

"I wonder, Dad." She shakes her head and shakes her head. "I'm afraid that in a year he'll be this kid in a yarmulke."

"Do you see me wearing a yarmulke?"

"You know what I mean. Expecting him to *read* all the time. Forcing piano lessons on him, the way you did on me. I want him to be my nice free American kid. Anyway, Richard wants this. So we're going to try."

It's a Tuesday morning in early June. Gershom arrives at the minyan a few minutes late and hurries to catch up — to wrap himself in the tallis and strap on his tefillin. Sam says good morning, Kate says good morning. Nick Shorr, Executive Director at the synagogue, says *Boker tov.* "So — where's the grandson? No Kyle?" Sam asks.

"He's with his mother in New York. She couldn't stand it anymore, being away from him. We'll see how long that lasts. We'll be going down this weekend for Kyle's seventh birthday."

Back to prayers. But Kyle's beautiful face comes between Gershom and the prayers. The boy will be back to his violent computer games and the foolish apps on his smart phone. Where there could have been depth in his life, at least a mix of cultures, of values, there'll be only — all right, all right! — if he's judgmental *let* him be judgmental — the emptiness, the vulgarity of popular American culture. It's lose-lose. Eve will focus on the glamor of personal success. On display! And he and Susannah will be without the child and the life energy he brought. They'll visit back and forth, but not enough to help Kyle's soul flower. But ahh, who's to say? Who's to say his soul won't flower while he's with his mother? Who's to say Kyle won't help his mother grow?

And after all, it's partly his own fault — making Eve feel it's her obligation to take Kyle.

He prays for Eve to grow up.

And prays that his stiff, judging heart can soften.

* * *

A Question of Heart

ALEX KOENIGSBERG, Professor of Jewish Studies at Tufts, is in exile—an exile he's accepted—as Abraham accepted exile, he thinks (wanting to give his life a nudge toward dignity). In his Edwardian with its white clapboards a mile away, a house he put so much work into, Carol, his ex of thirteen years, is living with a man who had once been Alex's close friend. For almost two years Alex has lived alone in a condo near Brookline Village. Vinyl clapboards, walls like enormous speakers through which he can hear neighbors fight and make love.

A man without a wife, it says in Talmud, is only half a person.

But he's forty-five years old. Busy with his research on Medieval Jewish communities. No internet dating for him. Please! Sympathetic friends invite him to have dinner and meet someone "just fabulous." No, thanks. His avuncular friend and colleague Barry Driscoll has asked him, "Do you really want to live alone the rest of your life?" Alex shrugs. Yet now, two years gone by alone, secretly he prays for a change in himself. Ezekiel and Isaiah both say, "*Take away my heart of stone and give me a heart of flesh.*" Maybe soon he'll be ready for love.

He and his ex, Carol, are on good terms, though they squabble by phone about how to raise Natalya. Take, for instance, her Bat Mitzvah. He wants a beautiful, spiritual life-event; Carol wants an extravagant, fun party for teens. But little squabbles with her he expects. What's been worrying him is Emma Driscoll. Emma and her father, Barry.

A little over two months ago Barry Driscoll, Alex's colleague in History, stopped in at Alex's office. Barry is the department's expert — a world class scholar — on modern European history.

"Alex? Got a minute?"

Alex waves him to the only chair not piled high with books. Barry unconsciously tilts his head, as always, so he can read the titles of books on Alex's floor-to-ceiling bookcases, English left to right, Hebrew right to left.

Driscoll is one of the faces you often see on public television offering background on the latest riot or a deepening of unemployment or a flight of emigrants through Eastern Europe or an outbreak in Hungary of right-wing nationalism. A handsome older man with wavy silver-white hair and a rich baritone voice: ah, television loves the guy.

But Barry is deeper than that. Alex admires Barry's intelligence and feels tenderness toward that deeper self. Alex knew Barry Driscoll's work years before they became friends. Driscoll published in mid-career three acclaimed biographies of modern figures. Alex had read his book on

Ataturk. Alex admires the power of his writing, his vigor, his insights—likes to listen to him speak about Ataturk or Trotsky or the young Churchill; and Barry likes to be admired—as did the subjects of his biographies. Well, who doesn't? But Barry doesn't puff himself up. Even on television he doesn't pontificate. He's canny, knowledge-able, without posing as someone who knows everything for sure.

"It's about Emma, you see," Barry begins. Emma, now in her thirties, is Barry's daughter with Nan, his second wife.

Alex supposes that Barry, so much older than his daughter, is asking advice of a younger man. At seventy, Driscoll is twenty-five years Alex's senior. He's been a mentor; but gradually since Alex came to Tufts fifteen years ago, fresh doctorate in hand, they've gone beyond that to build a friendship. Alex is pleased Barry's asking something of him.

Barry, his hair a shining white brush cut, seems much younger than seventy. He's still enlivened by teaching, stays very fit, runs 10k races, plays squash once a week, often with Alex, who really tries to win—though, admittedly, without smashing the ball too hard. Especially since he's moved into his condo, Alex has often been at their house; sometimes he's brought Natalya along. Barry's daughter Emma is not often around. She was there often as an undergraduate, but the last few years Alex has hardly seen her.

Now Barry ponders, ponders, floating in Alex's sea of dusty books.

"Emma's been nothing but a joy for us," Barry says. "She's been a loving, faithful daughter to her mother and me."

Alex smiles.

"What? What's that grin mean?"

"Barry, I really love your old fashioned expressions of virtue. A *loving, faithful daughter.* God knows I'm not making fun of that language; I honor it. It's who you are. So — what about Emma?" Alex knows she teaches sociology as an adjunct at Boston University. And she writes feature articles about rising third world countries and education, especially for women.

"There's something that seems to obsess her recently. It's in your bailiwick. She's thinking of focusing her doctoral work on Jewish communities in tension, her dissertation on Ashkenazi Jewish women in the nineteenth century."

"Really! You want me to help her with bibliography?"

"There's more. If she simply turned toward Jewish Studies, well, that would be — let me be straight — a little odd, out of her field. As if you, a Jew, decided to study Anglo-Catholicism. Still. . . reasonable, acceptable — perfectly okay. I mean to Nan and me."

"*But?*"

"*But* she's also, she tells us, thinking of converting."

"Converting to Judaism? And would that bother you?"

"Well, I'd find it odd, frankly. Every time she's been with us lately, she's talked about it. At first I thought it was merely to make family dinner table conversation more exciting. To pull my chain. But I don't think so. Now. Emma's had a hard time. A man she was with for a number of years. That's over, thank the Lord. But I wonder if Judaism is some kind of escape. Wiping away the past. She won't say. The lady's got a will. I can't tell her what to do. I wouldn't dare try. But why Judaism? Why not, say, Buddhism? As far as I know — tell me if I'm wrong, Alex — Jews don't try to make converts. Unlike Christians."

"We've not encouraged conversion, at least not for the past two thousand years. The traditional answer to your question — though it's not often practiced — is that the rabbi should turn away, turn away again, turn away three times, the person who comes seeking conversion. You can imagine perfectly sensible reasons historically."

"Of course. You were already being slaughtered as poisoners of wells, despised as money grubbers and Christ-deniers."

Alex laughs. "Right. Imagine if we went looking for converts! And if conversion's easy, will it last? Nowadays we question but don't discourage conversion — provided converts study, provided their life has become Jewish. At least that's the ideal," Alex goes on. "Of course, we've all seen intermarriages, where one partner 'converts' for the satisfaction of a family. But I'm speaking about real conversion. When we do accept a convert, we accept her, accept him, all the way. Oh, some accept as legitimate only an Orthodox conversion. And some never accept, but who cares about such people? We give the convert a mythic Jewish lineage. Her parents are still her parents, but we call her a child of Abraham and Sarah. We imagine that her soul was present at Sinai."

Barry interrupts. "Here's the point," he says, wiping away Alex's words with a wave of his hand. "Look. Emma talks about conversion. You speak about the need for study first. I'd trust you to do the best by her. You—you're a scholar. More knowledgeable than most rabbis. I've read your essays on Medieval Jewry, I've heard your students speak of you. You're known as a good teacher. And, then, Emma likes you. Don't interrupt—she does. So. If she calls you, you'll speak to her?"

"Of course. You *know* I will. But it seems odd you're involved. She must be thirty."

Barry laughs. "Thirty! Emma's thirty four. Almost thirty five."

"So she's a grownup. Excuse me for asking—but should you involve yourself?"

"Maybe not. Well, that's me. You want me to forget this conversation?"

"No. I'm glad to help. You know that. But tell me— you're not asking me to *dis*courage her?"

"Well, yes, Alex. Frankly, maybe I am. *If* you can do it honestly. Dissipate her romantic illusions."

"*If* they're romantic illusions. Isn't she too serious a person?"

"Alex, please—understand: I don't mean to put *your* beliefs down as illusion. For you they're a myth to live by. You're a student of Judaism, for Godsakes—pun intended. You've grown up as a Jew."

"Well, of course I'll speak to her, Barry. And if it does seem illusion maybe I can help her think about that. I won't *encourage*. I'll be glad to talk to her. All right?" Alex considers. "There must be someone she's already talking to. A friend? Or is she in love?"

"I'm only a father," Barry says. "You think she'll tell me anything?"

On the drive home Alex replays in his head the conversation. And winces. To be a mentor—fine. But in mind's eye he sees her: a beautiful young woman. And now that he's divorced—isn't it dangerous? Can he stay a mentor? *Sure you can. Don't be an infant.* Besides, he suspects she has a lover for whom she wants to convert.

No, no, Emma laughs as they sit together over coffee, no, she's certainly not in love. The idea tickles her. "Besides, do you think I'd convert just to be acceptable to a fiancé's family?" But as for friends?—Yes, she tells Alex, she *has* made good Jewish friends. "We've shared Shabbat meals, I've gone with them to Shabbat services in the library of an old synagogue, downtown Boston, first simply out of curiosity, then alone because, well, I found myself *moved*."

"And that's what's brought you to consider conversion?"

"Is that strange?"

"No. No. But it's hardly enough. Judaism is *one* beautiful path. There are others."

"That's why I'm here. To walk this path, to see if it's mine."

It's Friday afternoon. Alex and Emma are sitting in a Starbuck's near Harvard Square. He wants to play, from the start, the role of advisor. To keep that firmly in mind. Her eyes: she looks at him so directly, with such clarity, he has trouble breathing. He remembers the young woman he talked with fifteen years ago when he was a young, married faculty member and she a kid home from college. Now more beautiful as she's gotten older. Long and lean, soft light brown hair framing her face. And those eyes of hers!

"So. You found yourself moved. Can you say what moves you?"

She's silent, nodding. He respects the silence, going down into herself to come up with what's really there. Who was it called silence a safety fence for wisdom?

"For one thing," she says, "it was the songs without words—*nigunim*. Each time a *nigun* began, right away I knew where it was going and could sing it, as if it were already inside me and just had to come out. It can break your heart. You know?"

"Yes. Yes, I do know."

"We sing the melody again and again. I fall into it. Not knowing what it means. Not knowing why it moves me. Why I'm in tears. Not even caring. . . . And then," she says, leaning toward Alex over the table, "I've been meeting with friends some Friday nights at someone's home. We 'make Shabbos' together. I've kind of fallen in love with Shabbat."

"Can you say why?" he asks. There was a time, early in his marriage to Carol, when he felt he could live, they could live, in sacred space. That seems so long ago. But because it's so real and passionate for Emma, he's able to imagine that space.

"Why?" she says. "Because it produces a wonderful kind of peace. *Shabbat shalom.* It's different from an individual decision to be at peace, to find peace within. It's a community, a community *making* peace. I think it's beautiful that Jews can *make* peace through ritual and observance, make it happen, actually bring into being a holy condition, you see? — not from a connection to some disembodied spiritual world but within ordinary life. *Make* it, in the sense that someone *makes* a basket or a painting."

"Beautiful," Alex says. "Beautiful."

"Of course I know not every Jew is observant. Not every Jew makes Shabbos. But the ideal is real. To *make* holiness, make it right there. In ordinary life, in family life. With friends."

Alex nods, nods, listening to the music of her voice. When he used to see her often at the Driscolls, she was a friend's lovely young daughter. Now she seems suffused with, illuminated by, the resonance of her speech. She's becoming the teacher. Emma's scarcely older than his graduate students. She's ten years younger. He's never been the type to run after students. The truth is, he's never run after anyone.

"I know you want to do scholarly work in Jewish Studies. That's not the same as converting. A sociological study, an historical study—that we can get into by engaging in a study of texts. I'd be happy to do that with you."

"Tell me: What do you think is the difference?"

"Well . . . Do we study the lives of Jewish women in their communities or do we struggle to be close to God? A question of heart, of being part of a people."

"Ezekiel says, 'I will take away your heart of stone and give you a heart of flesh.'"

"Yes," he says. A shiver goes through him, for it's the words he's been thinking.

"My father speaks highly of you. He sees you as a person of heart. 'A man who strives for goodness,' are his words. He tells me that when your marriage broke up, you stayed kind, stayed calm. You refrained from blaming. He was impressed. I remembered how much he admires you. Of course I also remembered you . . ."

"He's a fine man, your father."

". . . when I was an undergraduate, I liked you. Thank you for working with me."

He's trying hard to remember the questions he wanted to put to her.

If, when he walked into Starbucks, he was scripted in the role of wise teacher, now he simply wants to avoid reducing himself, in her eyes, to a fool. "How do you feel about meeting with me every two weeks? If you can make the time, I will. I'll suggest readings, we'll both bring up questions. Questions to help you shape your dissertation. Or questions of heart. We can take the time to go through a whole Jewish year, holiday to holiday. The holidays are all part of a single story. And that story is a matter of heart."

"That would be wonderful. I'm not in a hurry. I'm not certain about conversion."

"Of course. You shouldn't be."

He reaches into his backpack, brings out a volume, a doctor writing a prescription. "Have you read Abraham Joshua Heschel? A good place to start." He feels heat in his cheeks—that cliché of bodily expression. *Take two Heschels and call me in the morning.*

"So we'll meet when I've read this?"

"Not the whole book. I know how busy you are. I've marked three short chapters." Then he adds, "And Emma, I feel *I* can learn working with *you.* It's a two-way street. If it comes to no more than these meetings, it can be good."

On his way home, he's feeling uneasy. It's the contrast between her father's expectations and what he actually did today. Discourage? Break down illusions? Hardly.

He wants her to convert, he acknowledges on the drive home, for otherwise, *how can he be with her?* Be *with* her? Fool! *You hardly know her.*

Again he meets Emma at Starbucks, not in two weeks but later the same week. They speak about Heschel, his passionate rhetoric. "He's a beautiful writer," Emma said. "But there's too much *God* in Heschel's essays—I'm very drawn to him," Emma said, "but I resist his high rhetoric. The music of his words pressures me to feel *God*. And the thing is, I *do* feel something true and holy, Alex. But I also feel Heschel's pressure."

They study one paragraph of Heschel's essay. But there's a unicorn sitting in the corner of the room, and it's hard to ignore the creature: He's not being faithful to Barry! He imagines Emma, the way the Song of Songs might imagine the Beloved, as a flowing hillside of golden wheat or as a mountain stream. He's telling himself a story. He imagines, in a kind of mental slideshow, children—his children with Emma. What a fool! After how long? A week!

At their next meeting they speak of Torah—how to read it. Should we consider Torah—the five books—as historical document? As founding myth? Why in the twenty-first century celebrate ancient agricultural festivals or care about details of sacrifice, rules of prohibitions?

"I want the heart connection we spoke of." She taps her breast. "Not all the rules."

"I know. But sometimes, Emma, don't rules generate creativity and express heart? Think of the form of a sonnet." He smiles at her. "Or think of baseball. Imagine playing baseball with no rules. Even to speak to each other we need rules of language. Rules let us express the heart and train the heart. Without boundaries, where are we? In Chaos-ville."

She looks down at the table top, and, with a forefinger, paints the shiny wooden surface with spilled coffee. "I've lived in Chaos-ville," she says. "It's not a pretty place."

He doesn't ask what she means. Eventually they'll speak of it, an ugliness in her life; he doesn't want to taint their growing close. But Emma's comment, its sad music, makes her more real for him, more strange, aware of how much he doesn't know about her. Not-knowing is okay. That there's so much of her makes her more precious.

They talk on the phone. When they meet the following week, she speaks — though he hadn't suggested it — about the Book of Ruth, Ruth's declaration to Naomi: *Where you go, I will go; where you lodge I will lodge. Your people will be my people and your God my God.*

She recites this. He becomes tongue-tied, fights tears. "Ruth the convert," she says.

"Yes. Not an Israelite — yet she's the ancestress of King David."

Has he kept professional distance? For a week he doesn't call; then she calls and they meet on the lawn by the Charles River near Harvard Square. "I've been re-reading the Book of Genesis," she says. "Some of the stories are so beautiful. Jacob meeting his wife, for instance. He sees Rachel, and that's it for him. He's on his way to his uncle's, his deceitful Uncle Laban, and he sees Rachel bringing her flock of sheep to the well — "

" — Yes," Alex says, "yes," breathing in Emma's scent. "And instead of waiting for the tribesmen to help roll the heavy stone off the well, Jacob does it himself. He must be strong as hell — powerful and motivated enough by seeing her to want to do it alone."

"And then he kisses her."

"It's not a Hollywood kiss," Alex says. "She's his cousin, after all."

"It's no cousinly kiss either," Emma laughs.

"No. You're right. And this love, it defines his whole life. And more — the life of the people Israel, this people you may want to join. She becomes the mother of Joseph."

"Love," she says, and shakes her head.

"Love," he replies.

They're silent, and still silent. Then, for an hour they turn from Torah; she tells him a very little about her relationship with Frank and its breakup; he tells her about his marriage and its breakup. It's so seductive, telling someone sympathetic a story that smoothes over contradictions, moral and emotional complexities. "Let's stop," he says. "Exactly," she says. They sit, look at the river. Eights from B.U. and Harvard row past them.

"I'd like you to meet my friends," she says.

"I'd like to meet them. They must be wonderful— they've impressed you deeply."

For awhile, he doesn't mention Emma to Natalya. Then he does. She's twelve, almost thirteen. She lives with him alternate weeks. One afternoon he watches Natalya at dance practice; after, he takes her out for tea. She takes her ballet seriously; she's been *en pointe* for a year. Her picture, a color photo, framed, sits on his night table. Ballerina of twelve, the camera has caught her mid-air in a grand jeté. Seeing it, every time, he's uplifted. Sometimes as he looks at the picture, he assumes her position as best he can while staying on the ground. Her teacher says she's a natural. Soon she'll become a Bat Mitzvah, and to keep the peace with Carol, he'll have to spend a lot of money. But her Bat Mitzvah won't be all party favors. He's been helping her, listening to her chant Torah, chant Haftarah. So busy, Natalya—practice and practice, then homework.

"You remember Emma?" he asks Natalya over tea and cookies, casually as he can. "Emma Driscoll? You've seen her at the Driscolls. You like her?"

Natalya dips a cookie into her tea. "She's cool. Uh huh. I like her. Why?" She gives a little shriek. "Dad!" She looks around the tearoom and asks in a whisper, "Are you going out with Emma? Are you *dating*? Omigod, you are! You're *dating!* And you're blushing! You are *blushing!*" She laughs and pops the rest of the cookie in her mouth.

"Not exactly going out. Or 'dating.' We talk about Judaism."

"Yeah, right! It's truly okay with me, Dad."

One night Emma drives over from Cambridgeport. He meets her at a bar on Commonwealth. A bar! Why a *bar*, for godsakes? Well, because it's dim, with posters from *Casablanca* slapped up on the walls. Because when he was here last time, it was quiet. Because he hopes to change the mood away from study. He'd felt that a drink might ease them both. It doesn't. Tonight noise floods the place, waves of laughter from a tide of B.U. students. A baseball game on several big screens is driving him nuts.

Some dumb place to have chosen! They lean their heads almost together to be heard. They talk about *Shavuot*, originally an agricultural festival but later a celebration of the gift of Torah at Sinai. They can barely hear one another. And besides, don't they have another agenda? Oh, they *do* have another agenda. She places her hand on the table; he covers it with his own. It reminds him of when he was a kid, say sixteen, and went with a girl to the movies, and it took him half the movie to put his arm around her.

Both stare at the hands, as if they were extraordinary creatures, separate from their owners. He releases hers. They laugh. When their eyes meet, they stop laughing.

"When I was in college," she says, "all those years ago, I had such a thing for you. I have to admit—that's why, when my father suggested you, I couldn't refuse."

He's glad the light's too dim for her to see his face.

One night they stroll down Commonwealth, couple of college kids on a date, to a little pizza place — three empty tables in an ugly, fluorescent-lit space smelling of crust and hot cheese. There's the ring of the phone and the loud repetition by the Middle Eastern baker of ingredients the customer asks for, addresses, the commotion as one of the two drivers rushes out to his car with the pies in insulated boxes or rushes in to get the next orders. But Alex and Emma are in a pool of quiet.

She says, "I was reading 'Song of Songs' today. Oh my. What I want to know is, what's a beautiful, sensuous poem, a love poem, doing in the Bible?"

"Rabbi Akiva once said, two thousand years ago, 'All the writings are holy, but the "Song of Songs" is the Holy of Holies.' He's perhaps the one who got it into the canon." Alex closes his eyes and chants a few lines in Hebrew, then in English, "'O give me the kisses of your mouth, for your love is more delightful than wine.' You tell me, Emma: How could a great rabbi and scholar praise such a poem?"

"Oh," says Emma, "sure. He thinks it's allegory. It doesn't read like allegory."

"The love of God for the people Israel, love of Israel for God. That's what we're told the poem 'means.' But why read it only one way? It's also a great love poem."

When he's alone, closing his eyes, he sees her warm, dark eyes seeing him. She's lanky and classically beautiful; he's certainly not. His black curly hair receding, he's a few pounds overweight. *But strong as an ox,* he says in his own defense, as if someone were evaluating. He pats his chest. A chunk of a man, a hairy creature. Hair on his chest and hair on his back. One night Emma said, "You know, I think you're a handsome man. You grow on a person."

He laughed. "Who, me?"

"You should use me as your mirror," she said.

Since then, he occasionally closes his eyes and sees Emma and repeats in his head, in her voice, *I think you're a handsome man.* One day, underground on the MTA, he looks at his reflection in the subway window against the dark of the tunnel. *Who, me?*

Soon, every day they speak on the phone or meet to talk. He grows more and more uneasy. What is he? — what kind of friend to Barry? A faithless friend. *But,* he offers in defense against an invisible Barry, *What about love?* Well, what *about* love? Is it really Barry that stands against them? Or his own timorous heart?

"I find I think about you all the time," he whispers into the phone. Then silence, long, long, they listen to the static. Finally: "What will your father say about us?"

"He may be upset at first," she says.

"I'm supposed to discourage you."

"You've failed."

"*I haven't even tried,*" he whispers into the phone. Sitting in his kitchen, preparing tomorrow's graduate class in Hasidic thought, he feels like a betrayer.

When they meet the next night, everything seems to happen by itself. She doesn't ask him back to her place; he doesn't ask if he can come. There's no need to ask. Holding hands, they leave their coffee shop and drive in her car to the other side of the Charles. He follows her upstairs: a slightly beat-up row house; Emma has the top two floors. They shut the door behind them; she bolts it and turns to him, arms open. He's trembling. They kiss, kiss gently, still they don't speak; he follows her to the bedroom. She turns and laughs a little, and, arms open, she takes him in.

Alex and Emma part from their clothes in slow ritual, become naked to naked in her bed and take a long time laying out the terms of their encounter, he touching, she touching, slowly entering, being entered. They dance together—it's dialogue, their subtle movements speech. A religious event, a communion. After, when they've groaned and given themselves up and half doze, there's such peace that it feels, he tells her, like a sacred time.

"What about the *rules*?" She's playing with him.

His fingers limn the line of her back. "It's a real question. Can we have a say in interpreting the rules? I think so, but I resist making claims."

It's two months since Alex and Emma first met for coffee. Today he drives his backstreet, shortcut route to Medford. The campus is flowering. On the way to his office on the Hill, he checks out Barry Driscoll's mailbox; it's empty. So Barry's in the building. Alex needs to talk to him. Alex is not ready to talk to him.

Barry's been a good uncle to him. No sneaky Laban. What's he going to say?

"Have you got time for lunch?" Barry Driscoll's voice on his cell, a missed call, Alex turned off his phone while he was teaching.

He leaves a message when Barry is teaching: "Faculty dining room at one. Okay?"

It's a cold, sunny day, but in Alex's heart the sun is a fraud. Tonight it's maybe going to snow. In April! Absurd. A chill wind makes a joke of his spring parka. Alex rehearses and rehearses meeting Barry, but, every time, he has to erase and revise, erase and revise. Every revision, as he walks across campus, ends in Driscoll furious, raging, threatening. The end of a squash friendship, the end of deeper friendship, of mutual intellectual respect. All right, not castration — like the medieval scholar Peter Abelard, who loved his student Heloise — but bad enough. *I expected better of you,* Driscoll growls inside Alex's head. What can Alex reply?

Instant dramas twist through him as students pass by, depressed or laughing, skate-boarding to class, the dramas all lead to shame. He deserves to be shamed. *No!*

Not so, not at all! I love your daughter.

What kind of friend? A betrayer! He imagines Driscoll saying. *I don't know what Nan will think.* Even worse, he imagines Driscoll saying, *Is this an example of your Jewish ethics?* Now Alex is mad — mad at himself, at the Driscolls. *Love!* — he says, weakly, in defense. "*What about love?*" he says aloud, just as he's passing a lovely Asian girl who was in his class last semester. She smiles, must figure he's on a cell phone. He's almost too guilty to smile back: *You wouldn't smile at me if you knew what kind of man I am.*

Driscoll is waiting for him at the entrance to the dining room. Alex can't think about food. "I'm not all that hungry. Let's take a walk, Barry."

"Sure."

In silence they walk the campus. Grass greening, promising that even New England, so cold and gray this past winter, will bloom. They stop at the Tufts fiberglass statue of Jumbo the elephant in a space defined by hedge, and Alex says, pointing, "Here's your next biography. Jumbo the Elephant! Oversized — like Ataturk and Churchill."

"Do I sense just a little hostility?"

"No. Envy. You know I admire your books very much . . . I admire *you* very much."

"But you think I identify with these larger-than-life men? Maybe it's true. My next book is about Admiral Nelson. Well, what I feel about you, if we're being honest here, is that you won't allow yourself to be as big as you can be." He squeezes Alex around the shoulder. "Now. My daughter. Tell me," Barry says, "how's the teaching coming along?"

"Fine, fine. She's a person of great depth."

"She is. And have you discouraged her from conversion?"

"I still can't predict what will happen."

Infuriatingly, Barry lifts his eyebrows. "*I* can." Then: "Come for dinner Friday night. Emma will be there. You can bring candles and light them and bless the wine. Emma will like that."

"I'll be there. I'll bring Natalya. It's our time together. Okay?"

It's a grand house in Newton with a staircase rising from the hall to a landing, then up to the second floor, the kind of staircase brides descend, floating down to music by Mendelsohn, white train trailing, in old black and white movies. Natalya cries out, in ascending pitches to whoever's there, "Hello, hello, hello!" as she always does. In a cloth bag, Alex carries candles, a bottle of wine, a challah. He kisses Nan. He has a mad, momentary fantasy of converting the whole family while he's at it! Nan, ardent Episcopalian, Barry, atheist, and of course Emma. And what about her half-brother, a lawyer in Chicago? Sure, we'll convert him, too. And has she got cousins? Reb Alex will take them all on! We'll all sit around the Sabbath table.

But first, a lighting of Shabbat candles, a blessing over

the wine, over the bread. God be praised — praised however we imagine the unimaginable for which we yearn. *Like a stag crying for water / my soul cries for you, O God.*

Emma hums a nigun, song without words, for the Sabbath; Alex and Natalya join in. Then he sings in his rough voice and translates "Shalom Aleichem" — *Peace be with you.* Sitting beside him, Emma touches his hand under the table.

Alex and Barry clear the dishes, and Alex tugs at Barry's arm. "We need to talk."

They retreat to Barry's study, history on shelves surrounding them. Out of place, tall aluminum frames attached to large canisters holding flood lights, lean against the wall in the corner. Barry points, laughs. "I'm being interviewed in the morning for a WGBH program — Turkey as a secular state."

Alex nods. In a stiff chair he waits for Barry's attention; Barry takes his sweet time, sits in a leather recliner, leans back.

"The thing is," Alex says, "I'm in love. With your daughter. I'm in love with Emma."

Barry frowns; all the wrinkles of his face deepen. Then, ah, then, his face opens in a huge smile. "He's in love, my young friend is in love. Congratulations."

Alex's almost angry. "You don't get it." He puts his hand over his heart. "I don't mean I'm *fond* of Emma. I mean I love her, I'm deeply in love with her."

"I know. Well, well. These things do happen," Barry

Driscoll says. "Yes, they do."

"'*These things do happen?*' What kind of banality is that? I committed myself to be a mentor. And to discourage her. You asked me to discourage her, didn't you?" Alex looks at his friend. "Didn't you?" From the kitchen the far-off clatter of dishes, shrill laughter—Natalya, Emma, and Nan. Alex peers into Barry's eyes. Barry's eyes are bright, his smile big, very big. Oh, is he amused.

And Alex *gets* it. Gets it! "Why, you trickster! You—you've been playing me, conning me, haven't you? What a dumb fish I am. You knew, didn't you—you set it up. It was your plan all along!"

"Not a *plan* exactly. Alex, how could I make a *plan*? It was up to the both of you. I just set up the conditions. The possibility. You—you're so timid, my friend. You know what I think? I think you used me as a way to protect yourself. You're a timid lover. But I believe you'll make a good husband. Now, you have to be big enough to *take*. Grandly. To rejoice in Emma. You may be, as much as Emma, undergoing a kind of conversion, young man. Take a risk. Open your heart. Why," he whispers, "perhaps you'll marry."

"What? And have *you* for a father-in-law?" Alex glowers. They laugh together. "You just wait, Professor, till I get you on the squash court."

It's love, just love, heating his breath, changing what he sees, what he hears. Fusing, diffusing, confusing everything. Later, when they're by themselves, he asks, "Emma—you think my role as teacher might get in the way of love?"

"No doubt," she says. "And love will get in the way of teaching. But there's something harder we need to talk about. Alex? If we're together, suppose I *don't* convert? Remember? We spoke about that kind of pro forma conversion."

He sat beside her, stroking her hand, nodding, nodding, not answering. She waited, patient. "I want you to be part of my people," he said. "Of course. Sure I do. But suppose you never convert?— even then I'd want to be with you. Marry you. Live with you. . . . It shocks me to say this."

"That sounds a lot like a proposal."

"It is. Will you?"

"Hard for you to say the words, hmm?"

"Sometimes I'm just shy with you." Heaving a breath, Alex rolls the stone off the well: "Emma, Emma, will you marry me?"

"Oh, my," she says. "You've got it real *bad*, haven't you!" And she laughs and leaning over, kisses his cheek. "Oh, well. Me, too. Me, too. And *yes*." Closing their eyes, they kiss. In his own words, in two languages, he offers thanks.

* * *

The Gift

WHEN JERRY BREITBART'S FATHER, Bernie, died, almost the whole synagogue, B'nai Shalom, went into deep—not perfunctory—mourning. This was a good man. And who didn't know Bernie? Some years he was Co-President of the synagogue. To twenty years of kids studying for their Bar or Bat Mitzvah, he'd taught trope— the various modes of chanting the various prayers, of chanting Torah, of chanting Haftarah. He'd grown up in an Orthodox family in Boston, attended yeshiva. Liturgical Hebrew and melody were in his bones. This was his gift. He wasn't paid for this teaching—well, he hardly needed the money—but it was understood that the child's family would make a contribution to the synagogue. The kids came after school, a few each year, one at a time, to Bernie and Eleanor Breitbart's Brookline apartment. From the next room mother or father listened to the teaching or sat with Eleanor Breitbart and talked. Bernie challenged you; Eleanor was easy to talk with. Bernie was aggressive, Eleanor gentle. A little overweight, soft, her voice mellifluous. She hugged. She patted.

All the kids were a little scared of Bernie. Or no— *pretended* to be scared, enjoyed pretending he was this ferocious taskmaster with wild white hair and a temper, who, like Moses, demanded that you listen. His bolts of grump, his fierce judgments!—*What kind of practice do you call that? Huh?* But even his grump was kind. A kid would parody Bernie to another kid, "What! You call that practice? What's all the bumbling and stumbling? You dumsky! It ought to come off your tongue like wet noodles." And the other kid would wriggle his fingers in the air and go *wooooo* and pretend to quake in his boots.

Ah, he was sweet on them, and they knew it. They knew it and they'd work hard for a smile from him. His son Jerry, too. Jerry, now almost fifty, remembers: Godforbid Jerry should have anything but perfect grades.

"I should have been a schoolteacher," Bernie used to say. "Instead, I became rich. A good choice if you're not a scholar like Jerry here." And he'd poke Jerry's shoulder. Bernie was a partner at an outdoor billboard advertising agency and had made himself a wealthy man. In Boston he was called the Billboard King. "We're very lucky. Your father made a small fortune for us," Jerry's mother Eleanor liked to say.

After retiring from the firm, Bernie lived on investments and spent a lot of time at the synagogue. For a man in his late-seventies, Bernie, always an athlete, was still strong, swimming every other day, still playing a decent doubles game at the Mt. Auburn Club—his returns slow but well placed. Friends kidded him—You're the Gregory

Peck of B'nai Shalom. It's true. Look at the guy, he could pass for sixty.

You could see it in his walk—his stride—fast and powerful, and in his chanting, a booming baritone. When they walked down Newberry Street, Jerry was amused to see it was Bernie, thirty years older, whom the women eyed. Jerry is a fine looking man who keeps in good shape, but he doesn't emanate sparks like Bernie.

And then, three years ago, muggy day after a bad night's sleep—a heart attack. Congestive heart failure. Diet changed. Pills multiplied. Bernie got along, after the attack, on pure will. Doctors' receptionists rolled their eyes. He griped and charmed to get early appointments. He felt he had special permission to be "a royal pain in the ass."

Jerry, his son Jerry, didn't often come to services. He felt at home in the synagogue, knew the prayers. But "God is my dad's territory," he liked to say. Still, sometimes he came, mostly to please his father. And was his father pleased? Though he gave freely to friends and family, he begrudged giving approval to his son. If the children Bernie taught weren't really afraid of the old man, Jerry was. Bernie could be sweet, but he could also get ferocious, a roaring lion. Sometimes he'd yell and pound his fist to show how impassioned he was about something. Jerry, even as a child, would try to turn his dad's anger into a joke. But it was no joke. Growing up, then grown up, even now when, for godsakes, Jerry was fifty, he found it necessary to court Bernie's favor. To make nice.

To please him, Jerry would, some Saturday mornings, pick him up—they lived just a few blocks apart—and drive to Shabbat services. And then one Shabbat, sitting with Jerry in one of the old wooden pews the synagogue bought from a church going out of the holiness business, Bernie Breitbart, in the middle of singing a Sabbath psalm, stiffened and slumped against his son's shoulder.

The whole synagogue grieves. The fact that he died in the sanctuary has put the members of B'nai Shalom in a kind of awe: to face the mystery of life and death so directly.

Emails go back and forth. Services and visiting hours are announced. Eleanor and Bernie's apartment is too small for so many mourners. So the Breitbarts sit shiva at the family house—the house that *used* to be Bernie and Eleanor's—a sweet Victorian near Brookline Village. It's where Jerry grew up, where his parents lived until Jerry and Hannah had their second child. Then Bernie, in expansive mode, delighted to be the giver, argued that it made no damn sense to rattle around this big house. "I went out and found us a high-end co-op. A terrific apartment. Not far, a couple of blocks away. Good lighting, big rooms. So . . ." He held out his hands, palms up ". . .This house is yours. Okay?" A hard man to argue with. Jerry, Hannah and their kids moved into the house.

Jerry hides himself away, doesn't want even his mother, even his wife, to see him weeping, controlling himself, tumbling into tears again. His mother, Eleanor, says, "I need a hug from you," and he hugs, and they cry together. He's comforted: her softness. Their daughter Nancy cries; their son David, dry-eyed, takes charge of the food, the guests.

For two, three days there's a minyan mornings and evenings in the big house, services led by Sam Schulman, who's known Bernie for decades, or by Rabbi Stein. Even at 7:30 in the morning there's a full minyan of ten, enabling the family to recite Mourner's Kaddish. In the evening thirty, forty, take part.

The mirrors are covered with cloths. People bring food and more food. Bagels and cream cheese, crackers and humus, banana bread and Danish. A bowlful of grapes, green and red. Seltzer on the table, coffee in the morning, tea at night. Glass plates. No flowers. Never flowers. Where, Jerry wonders, did that tradition arise? It's good, it's right, he thinks. Spare. Like the simple shroud and closed pine coffin. Again and again Bernie had told Eleanor, had told Jerry: no hiding of the human condition in a fancy casket. Let the cost of a fancy casket go to Doctors Without Borders.

Mourners spill over the living room and up the stairs. Sam Schulman has brought boxes of prayer books from the synagogue. Most people know most other people. Jerry

and Hannah try to protect Eleanor from becoming over-
tired with talk. But talk, Jerry knows, relieves the heart.
There's a great weight on Jerry's heart. It's okay when he's
quiet, but it's hard for him to get out a sentence — telling
of some goodness of his father — without breaking up.
After the brief service Monday evening comes the deeper
work of the gathering. Jerry, a computer designer, and
computer architect, has set up a number of laptops, each
with the same slide show: Bernie's youth, his marriage to
Eleanor, Jerry as baby, the family growing up, growing
older. Happy events. Jerry's wedding to Hannah — Bernie
in the middle, his arms over their shoulders. The grandchildren on a boat with Captain Bernie; Bar Mitzvah, Bat
Mitzvah, Nancy's kiss for Grandpa. Jerry has folded in
pictures of some of Bernie's favorite kids from his tutor-
ing. As if he were an outsider adding up his feelings —
though he's part of the life in those images — Jerry, in spite
of being shoved around by Bernie's critical nature, loves
and admires this man, this kind man — for he *was* kind,
was always a loving husband and father, though he found
it hard to express affection in family without throwing his
weight around. Will I, Jerry says to himself, ever be such a
loving and giving man?

Rabbi Stein, gathering people into the living room,
says, a little too momentously for Jerry's taste, "A *life!*"
The grandchildren, Nancy and David, tell stories, friends
tell stories. They'd go on and on telling stories, creating a
larger-than-life figure, a cartoon figure, till Sam Schulman,

on a nod from Rabbi Stein, says, "It's time to go home, folks, and let the Breitbarts get some rest." He announces visiting hours, services. Saying goodbye, shaking hands, hugging, Jerry finds he knows almost everyone. But one woman he doesn't know, a woman maybe sixty, beautifully dressed in white. Her cheeks are wet and eyes red from crying. So it must be someone close. Jerry wants her to feel included, so he introduces himself.

"Thank you for coming. So. You knew my dad well?"

"Knew your dad? Oh, yes! I'm Margie Slovin," she says. "Jerry, of course you don't remember me, but when I was about fifteen and you were—oh, I don't know, maybe four? Five?—I babysat you. But I knew your parents already. Our fathers were good friends."

"Oh, of course—Leonard Slovin. Of course. I remember his funeral."

"Your parents were really kind to me. Your father, especially. . . . I can't begin to tell you what a kind man he was."

"Thank you, thank you. Yes. I know. Yes."

What is there to say?

He watches Margie walk across the clogged room and hug his mother. They speak briefly.

Margie Slovin slips away.

Jerry is restless, sleeps poorly; as he comes out of sleep, he hears his father's voice. The third day of sitting shiva, after morning services and coffee, mostly just to leave the house, Jerry walks the ten minutes to his parents' apartment, sits at his father's desk, and looks at financial statements. He knows his father would say, *You're supposed to be mourning your father, you shmageggy. What is this? Should you be working on money matters?* He can almost hear his Dad's voice—almost an auditory hallucination. It's as if the words are coming from his own chest; as if, should he turn to a mirror, he'd see his father looking out. His father has nested inside his skin. Strange invasion.

It's the desk, he tells himself, a very heavy, solid, antique piece of furniture. What a time they had tilting it onto the hand truck and rolling it through the big house, down the front steps, into the truck, then up to the apartment. Should Jerry have the desk brought home again? His mother won't mind. She's living with them during this time of mourning. Maybe she'll sell the apartment and live with them permanently. Even if she keeps the apartment, she'll want Jerry to have the desk.

Sitting at the desk, he becomes his father, and it takes some doing to remain Jerry. Jerry, after all, is not a powerhouse. Nor does he want to be. He's got a good life—a good marriage, wonderful kids. But the desk—the desk does it to him. He remembers so many times, as a child—his dad turning from the desk and praising him or, more often, getting red in the face and chewing him out. His father used to bang on this desk to make a point. Then sigh, smile, kiss Jerry's cheek.

He can still feel the kiss.

And there were times he fooled you. For instance, remember how nervous Jerry was when he went into the study after dinner — he must have been seventeen — to tell his father, "Dad? I'm not going to major in business. I want to go to MIT. I want to do math and computer science."

His father turned from the desk and heaved a big breath — a warning sign. "I've dreamed about you taking over from me. Don't you wanna be The Billboard King?"

Jerry sat on a side chair, ready to debate, but his father roared a laugh and reached over to punch his shoulder. "Kidding, I'm kidding. Last thing I want — for you to copy me! I'm proud'a ya. MIT sounds pretty damn good to me."

Of course, in the week when the family sits shiva, Jerry's supposed to absent himself from work as much as possible. But, he tells himself, sitting at the desk, it won't be that much work. Bank accounts, investments are in both his parents' names, so almost all the estate simply stays in her hands. Jerry pays bills and makes notes for the accountant, leaving sticky tabs for his mother's signature; he goes through his dad's checkbook, through folders stacked and labeled. Major Appliances. Charity. Summer House. Repairs.

One folder he doesn't understand: a separate bank account. He finds a list labeled "Monthly Condo Payments," a list going back for years, each month checked off — payments for a condo on Kent Street in Brookline. A double line. "Finished." Years ago, paid up. A copy of the deed. The name of the owner: Marjorie Slovin.

The file is labeled "Margie."

He laughs at his first thought. No, Dad's not like that. Dad had an impassioned but ordered soul. Last guy in the world to "keep" another woman. Margie Slovin? Thirty years ago she must have been a beauty. But what's that got to do with it? Of course there's a perfectly innocent explanation. After all, Dad hasn't hidden the folder. It's right there.

But . . . *my dad, paying for a young woman's condo? What* explanation? What "perfectly innocent explanation" could there be?

He's afraid of showing his mother the folder. He walks home and shows Hannah. "What do you think?" he asks. Asks in a whisper, though his mother's hearing is so bad he doesn't really have to worry. "Should I ask Mom about this Margie Slovin? Just casually?"

"Jerry! Absolutely not. Why start trouble?"

"You're right. But it really gets me." Jerry is used to listening to his wife. He's good in his work, he's good in friendships. He's a doer. But when it comes to being sensitive around family issues, he turns to Hannah. "Does this sound like Dad? It doesn't sound like Dad, does it?"

She sighs. Her sigh is more irritating than Rabbi Stein's. It's patronizing. It sounds as if she's playing Yiddishe Mama. The Hannah he knows is shrewd, clear eyed—a woman who dresses in business suits, who writes corporate reports for a living. That sigh sounds like there should be klezmer music on the sound track. This he hates. "You've always so idealized your father," Hannah says, admonishing with upraised forefinger. "I've said nothing. Bernie was a very decent human being. I've always admired him. He sometimes got crabby but the crabbiness became a joke. A man with a good heart. Why pretend he's a saint? Why do you need that? You know what? Good people do crazy things."

"*I* don't," he says. "Not like that. Do I?" He laughs a comic-sinister laugh. "Would you be so tolerant if I did . . . crazy things?"

A harsh, honest Hannah laugh. "I'm certainly not suggesting."

"I'm not a child," he says. "I know what goes on in the world. But my dad? Such a morally upright guy? It seems impossible. Do I know my dad?"

Now there's silence in the kitchen. Odd feelings he can't make sense of. A giddiness. He wants to laugh. Or is it to cry? Ever since Bernie died, Jerry has sat on emotional turmoil. He asks himself, What will it be like, folding Marge Slovin into my slide show of my family? Dad in a tallis, Dad kissing my mother. How fit in Dad with another woman?

A hot day, early summer in Boston. The first week of mourning, then the first month of mourning — *sheloshim* — is past; Jerry is working at the office again. On the way home — well, why not, after all? — spur of the moment, he decides to stop and see Margie. All right—not really spur of the moment, for he brought the folder with him to work today. He drives up Beacon and turns down Kent, stops by the narrow, brick-fronted house on Kent. Margie has, he knows, the second floor. From the street he looks up to what must be her big bay window. He hasn't called in advance. He hasn't known what to say. It won't be easier in person. But he'll say he's brought the folder. *Here, take this off my hands. It's yours.*

After all, the condo is in her name, though paid for by Dad. It's okay, he'll tell her: whatever your arrangement was, it's okay.

She stands, one flight up, at the door to her apartment. She's wearing jeans and a painter's smock, smeared, speckled with colors, over a man's shirt. Her gray hair spills out from her kerchief, fringes her long, bony face. She dabs a cloth with turpentine, wipes her hands. "Jerry. What a nice surprise. Come in."

"I was in the neighborhood."

Walk into that apartment, it's like walking into an art installation. He's enmeshed in color. Paintings—pastels, oils—on easels, on every wall. Painter's drop cloth on the floor.

"Will you have some tea? I've just heated the water. We'll sit in my little parlor—this room, I know, it must make you dizzy."

It does! There are paintings stacked against walls. He walks after her through a forest of brightly colored abstractions with hints of landscape. Within the land-scapes, half-hidden faces, ephemeral, delicate—human and animal—buildings, a river at high water. The canvases are full of energy. "I like your work," he says. It does make him dizzy; he does like it.

Then into her parlor: so different. You enter silence, peace.

He sits in a wing-backed chair, strokes the velvet as if it were a cat as she goes off to make tea. Already, knowing nothing, he's been rewriting his story of his father's life. So fast! Already, in the new story, his father has lived a second life, a life he, Jerry, will have to keep from his mother.

He feels the pumping of his heart.

The hypocrisy. It's the last thing he'd have expected from that righteous man.

He suddenly remembers. The painting over our fireplace! It's been there as long as I can remember. So much part of the house that Mom and Dad left it over the fireplace when they moved. A dreamscape with unicorn and phoenix. Margie Slovin must have painted it.

She's really talented, he says to himself. And what a strong face. Passing her on the street, all right, he wouldn't have noticed her; he'd have seen an ordinary nice-looking woman in her early sixties. Now he sees her as almost beautiful. Her hair cut short frames a long face, strong mouth, deep-set eyes. A face with character. Well. Dad had good taste. She must have been some lovely young woman around the time, thirty years ago, when the first payment got made. His face feels hot—what has he got to be embarrassed about?

It's that he's forced to see his father in a new way, is forced to be disappointed, ashamed. The deception, a shameful relationship, and with a woman twenty years younger. But there's something else he's feeling. For at the same time, isn't he intrigued? Doesn't he feel, just a little—it's weird, uncomfortable even, but there it is, let's be honest—admiration? Yes, a little admiration. Who'd've thought?

And something more. He's feeling a victory: seeing through the emperor's clothes.

She puts down the tea tray, the teapot and a little tin full of various teas. She's changed out of her smock, she's no longer dabbed in colors; she's again, as at the minyan, a woman in white—white blouse over her jeans, a scarf of white silk around her neck. He takes the folder from his briefcase. "Here." She looks inside, nods, nods, as she goes through it.

"Yes. I have the original deed. But you'll leave this with me?"

"Of course. It's yours."

"What a good man he was." She holds the deed and caresses it, as if it were a baby. "A beautiful man. I remember when my father was alive but very sick. This was fifteen years ago. Your father came and sat with him for days and days. He took charge at the funeral."

Now her face changes. It freezes. Until this moment, he realizes, she'd thought they were commiserating. Now she *gets* it, *oh*, and her face goes dead; she *gets* it. "*No*. Jerry, *no*. Did you think we were *lovers*? You did, didn't you? You thought I was his mistress? And this condo a gift?"

"I'm sorry. But am I mistaken? What am I missing? It's not a *little* gift, Marjorie. We're talking about a hell of a lot of money."

"What do you think he gave me? You think I let him pay for the condo? Oh, Jerry, you've got it all wrong. Go talk to your mother. Then you'll understand."

"My mother? My mother knows?"

"Of course she knows. *Certainly* she knows."

A long, uncomfortable silence. "Well. I'm sorry if I've embarrassed you." Puts down his teacup and stands up, doesn't look at her. She's saying something, he isn't listening. Being here makes him feel awful. He leaves the folder and is gone without a word.

Talk to my mother? At this moment he wants to hide what he knows from his mother. *Talk to my mother?* He keeps saying this on the short drive home up Beacon Street. He supposes he will have to talk to her. But how can he? He's afraid of hurting her—reminding her of what had to be some kind of betrayal. Yet Margie's surprise when she realized he was accusing her, it was real. Over and done with, maybe decades ago, but all this time there's been a secret in his family. Is that what disturbs him so much?

That he'll have to rethink his story of his family?

No. That's not exactly it. It's how he sees his father — that's the real issue. Past the moment of insane pleasure at unmasking the emperor, he needs his father inside himself — not as the grandiose emperor who told you how you should live and how you should think, but as the virtuous man. That's the father he needs, needs as part of his own best self. A legacy of virtue.

Both Jerry's children are away: his son David has gone back to the Jewish summer camp where he's a counselor, Nancy left last night for her Spanish-immersion summer program in Madrid. So he can speak freely. Home, he calls out, "I'm home, ladies." He kisses his mother and invites her into the living room for a little talk, while Hannah prepares dinner. He sits beside his mother on the couch.

"Ma, when we were sitting shiva, you remember after the service a woman spoke to you?"

"Which woman?"

"Margie Slovin. Leonard's daughter."

"Oh, Margie. Yes, yes of course."

He takes his mother's hands, as if to prepare her for something painful, difficult to speak about — difficult even if she already knows. On the glass coffee table he lays Xeroxed copies of the papers in the folder. "Mom. I found payments for a condo among Dad's papers. It seems he bought her apartment for her."

She doesn't register surprise. "That's right. Of course. He did buy it. Well, partly. Don't worry." Suddenly, just like Margie, she laughs and she puts a hand to her mouth. "Oh, Jerry! No! It wasn't like that. Is *that* what you thought? Is that why you have such a funny expression on your face? No, no." Now Eleanor calls out, "Hannah! We need you. Dear, come in. Come in, I want you to hear this story, and I don't want to tell it twice."

Eleanor pats the couch, and Hannah sits beside her.

"We're talking about Marge Slovin." Eleanor points to the pastel over the mantel. "That's hers. She gave it to us years ago. She's a marvelous painter."

"Jerry told me," Hannah says, "about the condo Bernie bought for her."

"In a *way*, bought. Partly. Let me explain. Her father, Leonard, was Bernie's closest friend. You know that. Bernie led at the funeral."

"I remember," Jerry says.

"Well, when Margie was a young woman just out of the Museum School, struggling to paint and make a living, she couldn't find an apartment with a studio. And she didn't have the money to rent a separate studio. As it was she had to take jobs and couldn't paint. So Bernie tried to talk her into buying a condo. He knew real estate. Well, this seemed impossible. A condo? No bank would touch her — a painter barely beginning to sell? And for whatever reason, her parents, Leonard and Sylvia, didn't have the credit rating to guarantee a loan. Well. We'd known Margie since she was a little girl. She was like our niece. She took care of you sometimes, Jerry, when you were little . . .

"Your father," Eleanor goes on, "could have guaranteed a bank loan, but he decided to lend her the money himself. It's the way he did things. He never told Leonard, never told Margie, what he was doing. Why not? So they wouldn't be so beholden. He pretended he'd negotiated the price down and found a bank that would give him a good rate of interest. He told her he'd handle all the arrangements. But *he* was 'the bank.' She signed papers, she didn't know. She believed, you see, that he was simply taking the bother out of her hands. Nice of him, you see, but she didn't know *how* nice. He did it, of course, partly because she was his dear friend Leonard's daughter. And also, he loved personal giving. He loved it. And loved to feel like a *secret* giver. Margie paid him by check, month by month, year after year. Sometimes — say if she sold a painting or two — she paid double, even triple, to build equity. Years ago the apartment became hers, nothing owed."

Eleanor is whispering now, as if somehow she could otherwise be heard through the walls and many blocks down Beacon Street. "Bernie gave her a chance to spend less time at a job, more as an artist. For awhile he also gave her a good part-time job in his Creative Department designing outdoor billboards. Later, just before she met her husband, she taught a little, and she took a job part-time with a gallery on Newberry. Your father was so pleased: With his help she was able to keep painting."

"What a wonderful thing to do," Jerry says. "Well, now the place is hers. But I don't get it. Why don't *I* know

Margie if she's been that close to you and Dad?"

"Well, we were *once* that close. When she was a young adult, we hardly saw her—just heard about her from Leonard. One time—you were with me—we dropped in on her show. Of course you can't remember. In her mid-thirties, she married, moved to London, rented out the apartment, continued painting. She's become quite successful. We occasionally exchanged letters. Then, we lost touch."

"I know how that happens." Hannah shakes her head.

"Now she's back, you see. Her husband died last year. Leukemia. Very sad. Very, very sad. And they never had children. So she's moved back to Boston. In the fall she'll be teaching at the Museum School and of course painting. We spoke maybe a month ago. She called to tell us she's back on Kent Street. I sympathized—about her loss. So when Bernie died, I called her up. I knew she'd want to mourn with us. But I've never told her the whole story about what Bernie did for her. It amounted to a gift of maybe fifty thousand dollars. It would embarrass her. She might think she should pay us back. No, I won't ever tell her. Of course, it would eventually be part of your inheritance, so it's up to you."

"Dinner's ready," Hannah says. "Some story. Some story. Someday we'll tell the children. Bernie will be a model for them. In how to live." She laughs and squeezes Jerry's shoulder. "Sweetheart—of course, I know, they have *you*. And you're a mensch."

"I'm not insulted. I should only be half as good as Dad. What a grand thing he did. I'll call her," Jerry says. "To apologize. Don't worry. I won't let her know the whole story."

From time to time that evening, he remembers his stupidity—jumping to conclusions. Sitting in what had been, during his childhood, his father's study—but at his own desk, board on file cabinets—he finds himself half groaning, half laughing at himself.

All of a sudden he stops. He puts his hand to his cheek. *Oh! I get it.* What he *gets* is something his mother doesn't know. This is really a comedy of secrets! Next morning, he calls. Fearing she'll hang up on him, he's been rehearsing a speech, but he's forgotten it. "Margie? It's Jerry Breitbart. As you suggested, I spoke to my mother."

"And?"

"I'm so, so sorry. I was such a fool."

There's a long pause. Jerry waits, waits to breathe.

"Oh, Jerry, yes, you were very foolish. It's all right. How could you know?"

"I should have trusted."

"Come see me tomorrow on your way home. Can you? This time we'll finish our tea."

And so he does. He leaves work early. Again they sit in her parlor. It's strange, he thinks, that while the large living room, a room that functions as a studio, is dynamic, turbulent, passionate, full of aggressive color, this room, this little parlor, feels so delicate, so faded, so old-world.

He invites her for Shabbos dinner this Friday night, and she accepts. He asks about her dealers, her recent shows, especially a retrospective at a London gallery. But there's something particular to be said.

"Jerry? You're wondering why I asked you over?"

"No. I'm not exactly wondering, Margie. I think I know."

"You know? Know what? — that Bernie helped finance this apartment?"

"No, not just that. No. It's that my father thought he'd fooled you so you wouldn't be beholden. But it's not true, is it, Margie? He didn't fool you. You're too smart for that. All that time — you *did* understand. Right?"

She nods. "Yes. Yes, I did understand. I knew what he was doing — helping me buy an apartment I could never have afforded on my own. I pretended to believe him. But Jerry, suppose I said to Bernie, 'Thank you for the almost fifty thousand dollars I know this is costing you.' He would have been disappointed. He needed me to be the innocent artist, needed me not to know what he was doing. That's what he was like. I let him pretend — that with his credit rating he could get reduced interest and could negotiate a lower price. I let him 'fool' me. Oh, it was good for me, of course, but my dear, Jerry, wasn't it also good for him? He needed me to be innocent, not grateful. *Taking* the gift, pretending I didn't know about money, wasn't that *my* gift to *him*?" She smiles at Jerry.

And Jerry smiles back. "Oh, now Margie, aren't you fooling yourself?"

"Am I? Maybe. At any rate, I accepted, and he told Eleanor, and she — why, she still thinks I was innocent, doesn't she?"

"And you want me to keep her thinking that? Keep your secret to myself?"

"I certainly hope you don't tell Eleanor I knew. But Jerry, now I can afford to pay you back over the next year or two."

"Oh, no. No. Let it stay our secret." He thinks for a moment. "If you like, think of it as *my* gift — a gift, if you wish, you can pass on to somebody else."

Driving home he realizes that he, too, has been given a gift. He's been given the privilege of giving as his father gave.

And . . . he's been given back his father.

He stops at Coolidge Corner for the light, and as he waits, light comes to him. He imagines back and back, generation to generation, sees rivulets of light coming together into streams, streams into a river; that's how gifting works, generation to generation, his father receiving light from his father's mother and father, from their light, from the generations before and before. He feels that light entering him, suffusing him, and he's grateful for all of it, for being in the river of light — light that streams through the long dead to his father, through mother and father to himself, and will go on, generation to generation. That's the gift, the light, from generation to generation.

The next day, a Tuesday, Jerry, needing to recite Mourners' Kaddish, goes to morning services in the small sanctuary at B'nai Shalom. There are six so far, but Sam Schulman says, "I made calls. Don't worry—they'll get here." Then he asks, "Do you want to take over, lead this morning in honor of your father, *may his memory be a blessing?*"

"Yes," Jerry says. "Thank you. Yes, I'd like to lead." He wraps himself in a tallis. He's hardly ever worn tefillin, but today he puts on the tefillin that his father left him. He plants the little leather boxes on forehead and bicep and winds the straps that tether him to—to what? To *The Whole Thing*—to something he thinks of, but would feel a fool to speak of, as the core of life. He remembers how much his father liked him to come along with him to weekday morning services. Usually he bowed out, and his father would shrug. *S'all right. Maybe another time?* Today he's happy to be here. This is that 'other time.' His father, his father's father, back and back, they'll chant though him. It's up to him to keep them alive. Though Jerry has avoided services these past few years, he remembers the weekday *nusach*, the melody for chanting that his father taught him so many years ago. And he remembers the Hebrew. Sam Schulman points out where he left off, and Jerry takes over.

* * *

Cleaning Up a Mess

SUSANNAH SAMUELS waits in the hallway at B'nai Shalom for the end of Tuesday morning services. Just after Gershom left the house this morning, she got the call from their daughter Eve, and it was so disturbing she drove to the synagogue to speak to him.

Through the closed sanctuary door she hears the singing of *Aleinu*, signaling the end of services: then voices, laughter. The door opens, a few congregants come out; half she knows well enough to nod to or speak to. She nods, doesn't speak, looks away. It's Gershom she needs; he's taking his time removing tefillin and tallis, putting them into velvet bags. He looks up; his heavy, wild brows lift. "Something's wrong?"

She shuts her eyes, rolls her hand in circles, as if she were splashing herself with water: Hurry, hurry! She waits till Sam Schulman, who leads morning minyan, has smiled at her and walked past. Now she touches Gershom's hand, speaks in a whisper. "It's Eve. She called. She was crying."

"That's not so unusual. I expected this."

"I know you did."

"Did I sound like a know-it-all? I'm sorry, Susannah.

So tell me. What's wrong, dear? Has this Richard fellow dumped her already?"

Tears fill her eyes.

He takes a deep breath and puts his arms around her.

Eve's husband Dan had walked out months before, leaving Eve a depressed single mother. Well, Dan was sooo boring, sooo tedious, Eve told them; in fact, she told them it was a Cinderella story. She'd been working in San Diego when she met Richard, Prince Charming, at a trade show for nutritional supplements. He brought her out of the boonies to New York to manage sales for his whole company.

Eve found a little apartment in the Village, but most of the time lived with Richard. Afraid he'd walk away if he were asked to take on the burden of a six year old, she left Kyle with her parents, with Gershom and Susannah — but then, when she saw that Richard favored the boy, she took Kyle to New York and found Janine, a graduate student in history, to be with him when she traveled. Which turned out to be a lot.

Gershom grieved at giving Kyle up. It's as if, Susannah told herself, now he could be the father he hadn't been when he was busy teaching and publishing. When Eve and her brother David were growing up, Gershom was often short-tempered, judgmental. And busy. Now, at seventy-five, he had time, he had patience. And Gershom felt he could give the child a grounding, a spiritual underpinning. Oh, Susannah thought, he was so critical of Eve! He felt Eve was offering Kyle no protection from the culture of computer games, smart phones, trashy movies. He wanted Kyle to know he was a Jew.

Susannah, Defender of the Heart, Gershom, Harsh Moralizer. That's what they were enacting. Foolish theater, she thought. Please. Let's stop!

Kyle stayed with his mom at Richard's or in Eve's little apartment with Janine. Richard liked Kyle well enough, she told her parents, but wanted him quiet, out of the way, a pet who made no trouble. Now, Eve told them a week ago, things have gotten uncomfortable — Richard, for no reason, irritated with her or with Kyle.

Susannah soothed and sympathized. This morning's phone call indicated a deeper rift. "She spoke to me for fifteen minutes. Again and again she broke into sobs. Dear? She *wept*. This is no time to be severe, judgmental, Gershom. She needs us. Our beautiful daughter needs us. I'm afraid she'll have a breakdown — the way she did in college."

"Just tell me one thing: did she also lose her job?"

"No. No."

"Well. Thank God for small favors."

"And it's not that they had a fight," Susannah says, her hand over her breast. "Eve said, 'He just seems tired of me, Mother. Tired of Kyle. He's started making excuses. Basically he got bored with our needs.' Doesn't that break your heart?"

"So exactly what is it she wants from us?" Gershom says.

"Dear? Do you have to say it like that? Really, *do* you? She wants us to take Kyle for the rest of the school year. Wait, wait, let me finish. Well. The school year ends in just a few weeks. But probably next year, too. Dear? You know how she can panic and make bad decisions? I suppose she should have waited till the end of the semester. But—"

"She's bringing Kyle before the end of the school year? What's wrong with her?"

"Actually, now, don't get upset, she's already on her way. She called from the train—the Acela. They'll be in Boston by noon. She couldn't sleep, so at six A.M. she packed and told Kyle she was taking him to visit us—isn't that exciting?—she bought tickets online. She asked for you to call her. She wants to make sure she has your blessing." She hands him her phone. "It's programmed. Just push *Send* when you're ready."

He holds the phone in one hand, rubs his cheek with the other. This cheek rubbing is the way he thinks—the way he's thought since she met him forty years ago. He rubs, he breathes as if he's lifting weights. "Didn't she tell us we'd turn Kyle into a little kid with earlocks and yarmulke? That she wanted him to grow up an American?"

"Oh, please. She *says* things. Now. Don't get grumpy. Will you call?"

"An American," he says. "What in hell does that

mean?" He sighs, stops. Breathes, surrendering. He pushes *Send*. She listens for his tone of voice.

"Eve, dear," he says. "You're talking from the train, hmm?"

Susannah can read—well, after forty plus years, of course she can—the exact meaning of his voice; she knows that no matter what words he says, Eve will be absorbing only the grim but loving quality of that voice—which, without *saying*, says, *How long are you going to remain an irresponsible child*? And Eve will try to sway him by offering up to him an image of herself as responsible adult, financially successful, showing him she's tired of playing the role of confused adolescent on meds. Susannah can hear her without listening. Yet Eve will also want her father to see she's a victim of this demanding Richard, see she's suffering, needing support.

Eve wants the best for Kyle. She really *does*, Susannah says to herself, as they walk down the echoing corridor and out of the synagogue, Gershom listening to Eve. They sit in Susannah's car, windows open this warm day. Gershom says, "Eve, dear. So exactly what brought this to a crisis?"—then is given no chance to say anything. Eve talks. He nods, nods, clearly bored—or is it anger covered by boredom—by Eve's narrative of pain and blame, till finally he says, "And how is Kyle taking all this? Can I speak to my grandson?"

But Eve has more to say. She's not finished. So there's more listening, and more, while Susannah watches her husband's face to ascertain what's happening, and he says, "Richard really said that . . . ? No, no, I *do* believe you. That's a terrible thing to say . . . . No, please, I *don't* want to hear any of *that*. Please. I'm not prudish, no, but you've got a child sitting next to you. Eve, Eve, shh. Can I speak to my grandson? Yes, of course we'll meet you. Back Bay Station, 12:03, sure, got it. Just relax, sweetie. Enjoy the fancy train . . . . No, no, I'm not criticizing your choice of train."

But of course, Susannah knows, *sure* he's criticizing. Sure he is. Even with her terribly high salary, Eve's always short of cash, happy to take "a little help in moving across the country," or "a little help in buying East Coast clothes" for herself and Kyle. Then why—Gershom must feel—*shouldn't* he criticize when Eve spends an extra hundred dollars or more on a faster train? Isn't he justified?

Susannah slips her a little help now and then: if an extra hundred dollars can help her feel a bit classy, a bit posh—a stylish professional—or if the cost of a pedicure can help her believe in herself, or if having her hair done, her beautiful, wavy black hair, makes her smile at herself in the mirror, then why not for heaven's sake? Where else is their money going? Their son David is completely successful, and she and Gershom have simple needs. Eve should be eased, coming out of a difficult marriage. Not easy to be a single-parent. And to be wooed by this Richard, then dismissed! So hard—the feeling she's unworthy.

"Did you like the train?" Susannah asks Kyle.

They're driving from Back Bay to Brookline.

"Oh, he did, he did," Eve says, answering for Kyle. "He loved it—except at the very end when he got bored, such a long train ride, and—" she giggles, "this little boy of mine ran up and down the aisle making noise and shooting people with his laser gun. *So* cute!" Eve turns to Kyle. "It was just *play*, wasn't it? So it wasn't nice at all," she says to her mother (making sure her dad can hear), "for the mean conductor to take the gun away."

"I got it back, Grandpa."

"Make-believe killing isn't good fun," Gershom says, "the way making tunnels from sofa pillows is fun, remember? And crawling through, remember that?"

"I'm faster. I'm the faster one."

"Much," he says. "Me, I'm an old guy."

"You're not so old," Eve says.

Susannah knows Eve told the story of the toy gun to get a reaction from Gershom. She's pulling his chain. She *wants* to play the role of naughty, spoiled girl—and for heaven sakes, she's thirty-four! But isn't it his fault, too, for accepting the role of judge?

Susannah promises herself she'll give each of them a talking-to.

But this afternoon, when she and Eve are unpacking clothes, putting Kyle's things in the dresser, she just can't do it. She can't! After years of therapy, she still can't stand squabbling. She needs to make nice. So it's Eve who sets the agenda. Oh, Eve groans, she was so *fooled* by Richard's charm. But the lovemaking—"You don't mind I talk like this, Mother?—it was really passionate, really intense."

She runs her fingers through her wavy black hair.

"But after a month of being together at work, being together at home, going through all I went through to find a graduate student as a nanny so I could travel, I could see Richard needed space, and really, Mother, I was prepared to give it to him. I sounded him out. I asked, 'Wouldn't it perhaps be better, Richard, if I stayed at my own little apartment with Kyle? Don't we need to give each other breathing room?' I expected him at least to say how much he loved me, but you know what he said? So disheartening. He said, 'You're right. But let's not stop seeing each other.' Not stop! Nice! Well, to go from a ten in intensity to a seven or eight would be reasonable. But it went down to a three or four. He stayed over at my apartment once. But then he started not answering my calls and emails. Except about business. And he was super busy at the office. I had to go back on my prescriptions, Mother. I did. Oddly, we were just fine working together—I don't understand it. I've done a great job for the bastard. He knows that, too. But he was dodging me. Emotionally. I knew it. I've gone through some disasters with men since Dan walked out. So I snared Richard in his office one afternoon—I was flying to Chicago that night—and said, 'Richard, really, what's going on? Are you seeing someone?' My heart was in my shoes, Mother. In my *shoes*. 'No,' he said, and I laughed, 'Well, that's a relief anyway.' But then he said, 'Well, I have *dated*, but she's not special the way you were.' Omigod! 'WERE.' I held back my tears till the elevator came, then in the middle of a bunch of strangers I began bawling like a teenager."

"Oh, my poor, beautiful girl!"

"It gets worse, Mother. Kyle, omigod, no matter how much I hug him and kiss him, Kyle squirms out of my hands and starts acting like a complete brat. He says he likes Richards's house and doesn't want to live in a small, cramped little apartment. And I know he's really responding to my misery, and I get scared and start yelling at him, which is all wrong, and he goes deep inside and won't talk to me. I'm scared being alone with him in my own apartment. Anyway, I tested him, I said, 'How about going to your grandma's and grandpa's for a long visit?' So here we are."

"Wait," Susannah says. "What did Kyle say when you asked?"

"Oh, you know kids. 'Good! Good! I don't have to see *you*.' *That's* what he said."

"Oh, honey. You poor, sweet girl," Susannah says. 'Can you stay a few days?"

"No way I can. In the morning I'm flying Logan to Denver for a trade show."

"Well," Susannah says very, very quietly to Gershom, her words bitten off, as, standing next to each other at the sink, they clean up dinner dishes, "It appears you've got your wish. Be careful what you wish for." Oh, she's dumping on him unfairly, she knows.

"What are you talking about? You mean Kyle coming to stay? Not *this* way, I didn't wish. This time, my dear, you'll see, we are going to have our hands full."

The hollow feeling in the pit of her stomach won't go away and won't go away. It's as if she were in a jet liner that, hitting clear air turbulence, drops fifty feet. And drops again. What is this panic from? It's not the fear they'll have their hands full with Kyle. Gershom's right, they will. It's Eve: Susannah fears they've done something fundamentally wrong in raising her, and now, well now it's too late. Eve may become a casualty.

Well. Not exactly. So many young people she's seen, kids of successful families, they're casualties — medicated or should-be-medicated or self-medicated on marijuana or worse. They live with parents or in apartments subsidized by parents. Some are in therapy, where they get a kind of diploma confirming their troubles. They're bi-polar, or just depressed; ADHD; borderline; even schizophrenic, Godforbid. Eve's different from the shaky young people they know; she has a good job; she's good at her work. But isn't there similar chaos inside her? She has to work so hard to keep afloat.

She wonders: is *Eve* medicated—beyond her prescriptions?

"What did we do so wrong?" she asks as Gershom sponges off the counter and kitchen table. "I mean—that she feels unworthy, unloved. Were we such bad parents?"

"Is that what she feels? Unworthy? Unloved?"

"She didn't say so, but I can see she's always judging herself, proving herself. Look how often she holds out her hands, palms up, and shakes her head. Like saying, 'I can do nothing.'"

"And you think that comes from me."

"*You*? I didn't mean just you." Susannah's lying and knows it. She changes the subject. "Tonight, after dinner, did you hear the tumult?"

"Could I possibly miss it?" Gershom says. "What was all that about?"

Susannah shook her head. "Kyle, screaming, poor soul."

"Yes, but why? I suppose," he says, "it's that he knows this time she's dumping him on us for a long time, flying off to Denver or wherever."

Eve walks into the kitchen. "He's in bed. He wouldn't kiss me."

"It's all right, honey," Susannah says. "You know how much he loves you."

"Isn't it better this way?" Eve says. "With you? He knows you. He didn't like Janine, staying with Janine. This is so much better. But tonight, oh, tonight was hard,

Mother. He wouldn't turn off the TV and he kicked and screamed—well, you heard—when I tried to turn it off. I offered him a deal—'If you turn off the TV, I'll give you ice cream and read to you.' He wouldn't even look at me."

"It's not politically correct to say this, but maybe, just maybe," Gershom says, "he needs a father who can give him clear boundaries."

"His father? His father is hardly strong. God! I'm a lot stronger than he is."

"I meant *me.*"

Eve laughs. "Sorry, Dad."

"Your mother thinks I judge too much. But I'm serious. Maybe he needs rules."

She sighs. "Oh, rules."

"You really need to go to Denver?" Susannah asks.

"God, yes. If I want to keep my job! And I do. Especially now. I have to show Richard how well I can perform—and completely without him."

"Mommy? Maaaah-meee?" Kyle howls from the bedroom.

"I'll lie down with him. See you in the morning before I go. Can you drive me to Logan, Papa? Or should I call a cab?"

Gershom has fallen asleep. Lying in bed next to him, smelling the faint smell of his warm shoulder, Susannah, too distraught to sleep, remembers Eve as a girl. Part of the trouble, perhaps, is her beauty. Maybe I made too much of it. Eve could always count on beauty. Her hair so long, full and shiny black, her strong cheek bones, eyes deep and set wide apart. Oh, but you can't pick beauty apart, feature by feature. Maybe she was beautiful especially because she always *knew* she was beautiful. Boys were tongue-tied around her. Brash ones showed off in front of her. She won the one beauty contest she ever entered, then refused the two-year contract for catalogue modeling that was its prize. When she played tennis, the school paper almost always had a picture of her, win or lose. Where did her beauty come from? Not from me, God knows. Maybe from some great-great-great grandmother in Kiev.

Susannah hears Eve packing in the next room. She gets up, puts on a silk summer robe and goes in to sit on the bed, watch Eve, and perhaps assuage her fears. *We'll take good care of your beautiful boy, and don't worry, I won't let your well-meaning father be too severe. Where will you be staying in Denver? We'll call you tomorrow night so you can speak to Kyle.*

"Oh, Mother, not just Kyle. I want to speak to you and Dad as well. And don't worry about me. I'm really, really good at what I do. Forget Richard. I don't need him. So what if he hasn't turned out to be the love of my life. He's given me an extraordinary opportunity. I don't intend to blow it."

"You're marvelous," Susannah says. "Soon, you'll be sending *us* money." Then she realizes, fleetingly, that "marvelous" is one of Eve's words. Once again she's been absorbed by Eve. She's glad Gershom's not in the room with them.

Eve bends down, a pair of red shoes in hand, and kisses her mother. "You, Mama, you're still wearing that awful old robe, aren't you! I absolutely intend to buy you a silk peignoir — peach, I think, to bring out your color." She plunks the shoes into her carry-on, sits beside her mother, enfolds her hands. "If Kyle becomes too hard for you sweet parents, just hire someone to help. You're so near Boston College and B.U."

"We'll be just fine, darling."

"I know that. Or else I wouldn't leave my darling boy."

Next morning, Susannah is awakened by Kyle, yelling. Kyle is running into the kitchen after Eve, yelling "Mommy, don't go, don't go, you bad Mommy!" As she puts on her robe, Susannah hears something thump against a wall. But soft. One of his stuffed animals?

From the kitchen she hears Eve: "I *have* to, you sweet boy — I'll be late. You think the plane will wait for your ma*ma*?" Susannah hates it when Eve says "ma*ma*," weight on the second syllable. It's so little like *Mama, Mom, Mommy*. As if Eve doesn't want to be *Mommy*. Not that she doesn't love Kyle. But to be a *mommy* is to be old — not young, sexy, and free. Oh, Susannah can understand. She blames herself: all the emphasis on beauty while Eve was growing up; on being valued for the looks that God gave her.

Susannah ties up her robe, hurries into the kitchen and tries to hold onto Kyle, who's clinging to his mother's business suit. Now Gershom's there, stumbling into the kitchen. He says, "We'll drive together and say goodbye to your mom, okay?"

Kyle's mad — won't look his way. Gershom lifts Kyle up and away from Eve and rocks him against his chest. Susannah worries about Gershom's lower back, but he manages. "Last chance. Wanna take a drive and see airplanes take off and we can say goodbye? And will you stop hitting me, please, mister? You think I like being hit?"

Kyle keeps thumping his grandfather's chest, but the thumping slows, slows, stops. He's sniffling. Now he lays his head against his grandpa's shoulder and rubs his unshaven beard with his forefinger. "We'll see airplanes?"

When Kyle was with them a month earlier in the year, he was something of a handful for Susannah at sixty-eight, for Gershom at seventy-five. But it's harder now. Late winter into spring, though he missed Mommy, though to be without her scared him, it seemed a treat — to be with grandparents who love him and have time for him. He was happy to make a tunnel out of cushions with Grandpa, to help Grandma cook.

Not this visit. He glowers, goes inside himself where Susannah can't reach. If she says, trying to coax him from his X-box, "Want to help Grandma with dinner?" he won't look her way. If she asks again, he snaps, "You can't make me. Mommy doesn't make me." If, when she picks him up from school, she wants to take him along to the Free Store at the Family Survival Center, he won't get in the car, won't budge. He stands in front of the school, arms folded. "You, you're not my mommy. You're not the boss of me."

He's six years old, but mornings his bed is wet. He and Grandma don't mention it. Saying nothing, she makes his bed with a rubber sheet under the cotton. He hates the slipperiness. Surprisingly, by the end of their second week together, he stops wetting the bed.

But at night, every night, they can hear him cry himself to sleep. At first she or Gershom goes in to comfort. Comforting doesn't comfort. Just sitting with him helps. One night she asks: Would he like music? He nods. She plays on his little stereo an adagio from a CD of Schubert impromptus. It repeats and repeats while she half-dozes.

The first day of school in Brookline, he won't eat, won't smile, won't take directions — or, even worse, he follows directions like a robot.

Later: "How was school?"

"I hate it. It's a stinky school."

Every day she asks; every day he says, "School is stinky." Finally, resisting the impulse to cajole, she laughs. "Absolutely stinky," she says. She sings along. It becomes a game, becomes their chant. *School is stinky, school is stinky.*

When he gets mad and Susannah tries to hold him, half believing that if he only let her hold him, he'd come out of this awful place he's in, he becomes limp, a dead weight. He slips from her arms. It reminds her of the passive resistance in which she was trained half a century ago, for use in protests against the war in Vietnam.

Which means she's like the police.

If it's easier for Gershom, that's because Kyle is a little intimidated by this lean giant with deep voice, six foot two in his stocking feet, with his deep-set eyes and bushy gray eyebrows. And Gershom isn't tentative around Kyle. "You finish your breakfast and I'll race you through the house," Gershom will say. "Okay? The rules are, you've got to touch something red *and* something green in every room. Okay?"

Susannah is a little scared of what's happening to Kyle. So she speaks to him—though she knows she shouldn't—as if he were a china figure balanced at the edge of a mantle. During his previous visit, the end of winter, when she walked into the living room where he was playing a computer game, he'd call, "I *got* him. Bam! You want to see, Grandma?" This visit, he doesn't look up. She holds back, afraid that if she asks about his game, he'll say, "I'm busy, shh."

Gershom won't accept *Shh*—he strides over, clicks off

the screen, takes—oh, *gently* enough—takes Kyle's shoulders in his hands, looks into his eyes and says, *Young man, I need help shopping at Whole Foods. Maybe you'll get a piece of chocolate out of the deal.*

Susannah recognizes that it's worse for her—because, she thinks, Kyle's made a transference from mother to grandmother. He tells Grandma how mean she is. Or how mean Mommy is. Or how he misses Mommy, or how he doesn't miss Mommy anymore. But sometimes—sometimes he sits on the couch next to Susannah and asks her, in the sweetest way in the world, if she'd read to him.

He refuses to talk to his mother; he demands to talk to his mother. When they do speak, he asks, "When are you coming for me, Mommy?" Susannah is hurt—as if she, his grandma, were a jailer. But she also realizes it's a positive sign when he's able to *want* his mother, not merely be angry at her desertion.

She pencils Eve's cell number on a 3 x 5 card Kyle can keep in his pocket; he calls her wherever she is—New York, L.A., Paris—calls whenever he feels like calling; when she doesn't pick up, he talks into voice mail. Sometimes at night, just before his bedtime, Eve calls Kyle on their land line. Gershom puts the call on speaker phone; Eve speaks more to them than to Kyle.

"Wait'll you see the fabulous rug I bought for my little place. I'll email photos."

"How's the job?" Gershom asks. "Are you still able to work with Richard?"

"Yes, I guess. But I think things are changing. He has a hard time speaking to me. I show him sales figures and he says, 'Wonderful. Hmm. Wonderful.' Then he avoids being with me; he hunts through his desk as if looking for something to say. It's unnerving. Is he just awkward because we had, you know, a 'relationship?' God! I was stupid to start up with him. But the job—well, the job is a wonderful challenge. I'm a great success. So. . . . Kyle, honey? Are you being a good boy for Ma*ma*? How's school, my Sweetie?"

"Stinky."

"No. No. You *like* school. You always liked school."

"No I didn't, no I didn't."

"You know what? My job is just like your school. I'm learning sooo much."

"Are you coming to see me? When are you coming?"

But Eve doesn't come. Their first Friday evening together as a trio, they light Shabbat candles, and Susannah sings the blessing, then Gershom chants the Kiddush over the wine. He lets Kyle take a sip. Kyle sips and makes a face.

"Kyle? Remember the blessing over the bread?"

"The challah!" Kyle says, remembering. They say the blessing together. At the end of Shabbat dinner, Gershom chants in Hebrew the first blessing of the *Birchat Hamazon,* the blessing after the meal, then recites the gist of it in English. "Blessed are You, Adonoy our God, Ruler of the

Universe, Who nourishes the entire world in His goodness, with grace, with kindness, and with mercy."

Susannah remembers that when they were first married, they used to chant the whole, multi-part blessing
at most dinners. That practice faded—replaced, after the
children were out of the house, with a few words of gratitude. Susannah knows that he loves rekindling the practice, teaching the blessings to Kyle. So now each night, not
just on Shabbat, Gershom chants, after the meal, the first
blessing. And Kyle, after a couple of evenings, hums the
music and mumbles the words he's picked up. Soon, all
of them.

And after Kyle goes off to assemble a Lego ship in the
living room, Gershom raises his teaching forefinger and
says to Susannah what he said during Kyle's earlier visit:
"To teach a child, a grandchild, it's the most important
thing."

"I know, I know."

She knows it will do no good to protest as she did
during Kyle's earlier visit, to say, *Isn't religious teaching
up to his mother?* Maybe, just maybe, she says to herself,
Gershom's right after all. *Up to his mother?* Eve won't teach
anything that will give Kyle a grounding in the world.
And for the first time, she says, "Gershom, dear? I take
back what I said about teaching. I think maybe he needs
you."

"Needs *us*," he says.

She thinks a positive change in Kyle starts from that discussion, when she and Gershom begin to work together as a team.

It's Susannah who brings up the idea of creating a chart. Gershom buys and brings home large poster boards and stores them away for Sunday. But he makes sure Kyle sees.

"What are they for?"

Gershom whispers: "It's secret."

On Sunday morning Susannah makes pancakes. At his most angry, most confused, Kyle loves her pancakes, especially blueberry pancakes. No. Especially chocolate! After breakfast—she's already spoken to Gershom, and he's willing—they all three sit at the kitchen table, and Gershom says, "Mr. Kyle, this is going to be a fun day. We're going to the aquarium to see dolphins and penguins, okay?" Kyle begins to stand up; Gershom plunks him down. "And right now, we have a family job to do. Remember the poster board? Ta-da! We're going to list all the things people have to do to be happy in a house. In *our* house. Ways for all three of us. For Grandma and Grandpa as well as for Kyle."

"Do we have to?"

"Nope. We can do it without you, but then you wouldn't get to use the posters. Grandma," Gershom says, "can you name one good thing we want for the three of us while we live together?"

"Mmm . . . . Laughing a lot and having fun together."

"Good." He writes this in a sharp pointed marker. "I'll say another one: Being kind to each other. Kyle? You say one."

He won't play.

Gershom says, "How about *yell* a lot? No? Then name something."

"Like . . . not make a mess?"

They put the ideas in rows on poster board, a row for each idea, a column for each day. The rows are for:

being kind to each other
laughing and having fun
cleaning up if you make a mess
learning new things
telling each other what we feel
helping each other do stuff.

Now, each evening, at Kyle's bedtime, they stand in front of the chart, which hangs on Kyle's bedroom wall, and decide how many points out of ten to give each good thing. If for *Cleaning up if you make a mess*, Grandma gets only a 6 (glasses left in the sink) and Grandpa a 5 (papers scattered on the floor) but Kyle gets a 9 (Legos put away), then the household gets a 20. You decide your number for yourself, but you can argue about someone else's number if you feel it's wrong. At the end of the week, you add all the points, see where we've all done well, where we've all done badly.

Kyle takes to the chart. In fact, he obsesses about the

numbers. "It's so simple," Susannah says a week later. "But it does seem to work."

For the household to get high marks, they all need to try. During the day Susannah keeps remembering the chart, remembering its categories.

By the next week, the household does seem a happier place.

Gershom begins to teach Kyle Hebrew letters. "This is learning new things," Kyle says. He smiles a satisfied smile.

He helps Grandma fold laundry. "This is helping our points."

It's crucial, she knows, to go to the chart every evening. Oh, she thinks, I wish we'd made a chart like this when Eve was growing up. I never asked a *thing* from her. But where's Kyle's anger? She knows it hasn't dissolved. But now he's talking to them.

One day after school, Kyle comes into the kitchen and says to his grandmother, right out of the blue, "Mommy would do *bad* on the chart."

"Did you tell her about the chart?"

"Uh-uh. No! Mommy will say it's stupid."

"Do *you* say it's stupid?"

He doesn't answer. He goes off to watch cartoons. Soon he's back. "No, it's not stupid. Can I tell Mommy?" Without waiting for an answer, he heads for the phone.

It's late June. Eve is coming for the weekend.

"Want to help me bake a cake?" Susannah asks Kyle.

"You can lick the frosting."

"And later this afternoon," Gershom says to Kyle, "we can pick Mommy up together at the airport."

When he and Susannah are alone, he whispers, "It mustn't happen again. Taking him back, giving him to us, taking him back. I won't let her."

She imagines a terrible fight. But she nods. "We won't let her."

He's silent. She knows how afraid he is. If he weren't there to express fear, she knows she'd feel it herself. *All our work. To spoil all that!*

Eve calls. Her flight is delayed in Atlanta. But half an hour later she calls to say they're boarding. Susannah aches to see her. She doesn't tell this to Gershom.

At Logan they park in short-term parking. Eve waves at them through the glass wall separating passengers from those awaiting them. Kyle and Susannah have made a sign on the back of a poster board: WELCOME EVE/ WELCOME MOMMY, and Kyle sits on his grandpa's shoulders, which puts him way higher than anyone, and jiggles the sign. Eve points at the sign and mugs laughter.

She's very high today. She kisses them all. Susannah worries: Eve's exuberance doesn't ring true. A social worker for much of her life, Susannah feels she knows when someone's false. Eve is bubbling, but the bubbles are empty.

"I've got so much to tell."

"I'm sure, dear," Gershom says.

Kyle leans over from his booster seat and kisses Eve's arm. Maybe this makes him feel too much like a baby, for at once he tickles her, tickles hard, and she laughs.

"My darling, darling boy! Look at him. Well, you've done wonders."

Done wonders. This gets Susannah's goat. She's never been comfortable at confrontation, but she has to say it: "Eve! That's what you tell a *hairdresser*, dear."

"Ouch. Sorry, Mother. I'm just so excited to be seeing my boy — *and* my parents. You can't imagine. I'll calm down." But at once she starts up. Reaching into her shoulder bag, she takes out of bubble wrap a framed photo from her last visit: Gershom, Susannah, Eve, and Kyle at the reservoir. "Look! Look! You see your mama? Be careful Kyle, my sweet."

Now she leans forward so Susannah and Gershom can hear. "My life has been changing. I'll tell you over tea. What I mean is *on the inside*. I've taken these *affirmation workshops*. It's made a big difference."

"So? What do you affirm?" Gershom calls back from the driver's seat.

"Every day, a few times a day, I say affirmations like these:

I am the artist who shapes my life. I am the builder of my own life.

I am full of energy and joy. I have been given great talents.

Love has taken the place of anger."

"And there's much more. You have no idea how it helps."

She quiets down. Maybe—for aren't her lips moving just a little?—she's saying her affirmations silently. Maybe, Susannah worries, we're making her nervous. Reaching back she grasps Eve's hand. "Did I tell you— you look just lovely. We've all missed you."

"Well, if I look lovely, I know why." But then, when Eve takes a deep breath and finishes: "I'm seeing my baby boy, *that's* why," Susannah is sure that isn't what she'd intended to say.

Susannah makes tea for them. She keeps exchanging glances with Gershom to see what he's feeling. She's afraid he'll blow up, say bitter things, there'll be turmoil, a fight, recriminations—which will do no one any good. The time she took Kyle back with her hurt Gershom so much. *Well, it hurt me, too.* The longer Kyle stays, the more Velcro—the harder to let him go. And this summer, oh, the work it has taken to help Kyle a little!

They sit in the screened gazebo out back. Eve has settled.

"Well, let me tell this my way, Mom, Dad. About a week ago, I get a call from Richard. Can he come over? Well, I really felt he shouldn't, but he's also my boss, and you know . . . . So he comes over. He's brought a lovely wine, *très cher*, and he opens it and we toast each other. And that's all I expected would happen. He's sitting across from me. He reaches out for my hands, and, get this, he's in tears! Omigod! He cried — my big, handsome man cried. He realized he loves me, he can't be without me, and so on and so on. It's embarrassing to tell you. So, we're . . . getting married! Kyle, can you imagine?"

Kyle's face is dulled. He says nothing.

"Your mama's getting married! You'll have such a fun pa*pa*. It'll be a small wedding. Mostly family. Don't you think that's best, Mother? In his sister's beach place in the Hamptons. And," she says, "we're going to live in his Paris apartment and in his New York apartment, as we need to for the business. And the business is thriving on both sides of the Atlantic. Nutrition is big business. Paris, New York, Paris, New York! Not bad, hmm? It's like starting my whole life over again. Erase. Rewind. Take two. And sometime soon, we'll take you with us, honey. You'll see Paris. And later," she turns to her parents, "when — oh, you know — when he can take the Metro by himself, when he's not so dependent, then it'll be different." Now she sits back and smiles at her parents. "You can see, can't you, it would be impossible, having him live with us *now*. You're happy for me, right? It's not so terrible for him, not with grandparents like you — I'm really lucky — and you've told me how much you want to be with him. We'll visit back and forth."

Sunday afternoon Gershom takes her back to Logan. Kyle refuses to go with them. Susannah can't blame him.

After "ma*ma*" goes, he's silent. He sits on the floor in his room playing with Legos. Oh, he did finally let his mommy hug him before she left. She said, "Kyle, my sweetie, you've *got* to call me. Call me anytime!" A kiss on his forehead; she and her overnight bag are gone.

Susannah is in tears from time to time. She wants to let go and weep, but she has to be strong for Kyle. This afternoon feels to her like the start of a long, long walk in a desert, lugging weights. Of *course* they'll go to the wedding, of course Kyle will be ring bearer. It's not an ending. Susannah can't help loving her daughter. Nothing's final. Eve will grow up. Or she won't. We'll still love her.

Eve a success? No. No. Just a different sort of casualty, who'll make a casualty of Kyle.

When she hears the crash, she knows at once what's happened. That photograph! Eve had placed it on the night table in Kyle's room. *Good,* she thinks. *Let him get the anger out.* Taking a deep breath, she goes in. Kyle has twisted the frame and smashed it against the wall. He's taken out the photo and ripped it, ripped it again. Pieces lie scattered. Susannah takes him in her arms. He's crying; he turns his head away but sinks into her arms. Oh—she sees he's cut himself. She takes him by his uninjured hand into the bathroom, tenderly washes and bandages the cut. "Now," she says, "let's go back in your room and clean up. You got mad. It's okay. We can get points for cleaning up a mess."

"No." He sits on his bed cross-legged, facing the wall.

Susannah wants not to let this be a big deal. On her knees she picks up the fragments of glass and paper, tosses the twisted frame into a plastic bag. She kisses his forehead. "It'll be okay. You'll see."

For now, it's not okay. He won't speak to his grandma or grandpa. Gershom pulls sofa cushions down to the living room carpet. Kyle won't join him. He won't eat dinner, not even dessert. To do so, Susannah feels, would be to compromise his anger. When Gershom calls out, "Time for the chart," Kyle says, 'Stupid chart,' and won't join them. "We'll skip the chart tonight," Gershom says; he looks defeated.

Kyle gets into bed without fuss. Susannah lies down beside him. "My dear, handsome, big boy. I know," she says. "I do know. I'm so sorry." She closes her eyes, thinks of all the work. She runs her fingers through his blonde hair. "My beautiful, beautiful boy. My sweet boy. I know, honey. I know." Exhausting! What will it take this time? A therapist? Medication? And on and on. Turning it over and over.

On Tuesday morning they wake early, walk on tiptoe not to wake Kyle. Gershom's shaving; Susannah sits over a cup of coffee. Now Kyle, his body still full of sleep, comes in, and she makes him French toast out of challah left over from Shabbat. Gershom stops in the kitchen, kisses Susannah, leans down to kiss Kyle, but Kyle sits stiff, a block of wood, picks at the French toast. She tries not to look. And Gershom—how gray and ragged he seems. Best not to speak about it. Middle of the night Kyle woke and called out; it was Gershom who rubbed his back and stayed with him till he fell asleep. "Kyle, dear," he says, "my good guy, good morning, honey," his voice musical, upbeat. Susannah hears the strain, feels what he's going through. "I'm off to synagogue for morning minyan. Some day, any day you like, I'll take you. Remember, I took you once?"

Kyle nods but won't look at his grandfather. Gershom leans over and whispers in his ear, "Listen, mister. We're on your side."

After Gershom leaves, Susannah takes Kyle by the hand, and swinging his hand as if they were strolling the yellow brick road, walks with him to his bedroom to pick out clothes for today. The chart is off the wall, she sees it hiding behind his rocking chair. At least it's not destroyed. Maybe, eventually, he'll want to use it again.

* * *

Whispers from a

Distant Room

A JUNE MORNING—air thick with moisture. The small sanctuary at B'nai Shalom, where the Tuesday morning minyan davens the morning service, is, today, a physical sanctuary as well as a space for worship. Passing through the door you go from muggy, heated air to clear coolness. Sam Schulman, Kate Schiff, and five others of the ten necessary to compose a complete minyan, have begun to chant when Peter Weintraub walks in, wraps himself in tallis and straps on tefillin. He's a little clumsy putting them on. Only recently has he worn tefillin, the black boxes strapped to forehead and left arm—inside, the tiny handwritten scrolls expressing the unity of God and the mitzvah of wearing tefillin.

At home he straps them on; here he's embarrassed— he often forgets to bring them.

What a funny bird, Sam Schulman says to himself. Says with affection. *A sweet man*. You never know when Peter will halt the service just after the reading, in Hebrew, of the psalm for Tuesday and read it again, declaim it as urgent communication in English:

> "Be just to the needy and the orphan, vindicate the poor and impoverished. Rescue the needy and the destitute and save them from the hand of the wicked."

Then he'll speak about the latest *wicked*: torture in one country or another, a story he heard on NPR about some dictator somewhere, some failure to consider suffering in our own country. "You see?" Peter will say, opening his hands as if they held the truth and the truth was so simple, so simple. "No man is an island," he'll say. Yes, yes, the other congregants say, but please, Peter, it's late, we have to get to work. Enough already.

Peter didn't grow up an observant Jew. This is all new to him, begun less than a decade ago after the kids were out of the house. At the end of the service Sam makes sure to say good morning, and Gershom Samuels smiles and pats Peter on the back.

And Peter bags his prayer paraphernalia, puts the bag in his backpack, and walks to Beacon to catch a trolley to work. He's frightened. He'd thought he was finished with what he referred to as "all that": the awareness that, years ago, opened within him like a crack in a wall. Look through at your peril. He lived it just a few months. More than a decade ago. He was fortunate not to have been locked away in a hospital. *In a way, Rachel took care of me in hospital at home.* Now, he's wary; well, of course. Who wouldn't be?

But last month, nearing his sixtieth birthday, as the old strangeness began secretly to bloom in him, bloom without his knowing, he wasn't wary enough — wasn't aware anything was strange, let alone dangerous. Why now? Is it that he'd studied *chi gung?* He'd learned to play with a ball of *chi* — the invisible force field he'd been learning to raise and move. Maybe this was a mistake.

Try this: simply imagine a ball in your two hands, too big for the hands to touch one another. At first it's just imagining. You roll the ball within the open sphere of the palms of your hands. You compress the ball, you enlarge the ball. You roll it, you dissolve it. And of course after awhile you truly feel the ball, a ball made of energy. Made of — what else? — your own energy and imagination. And something more? But now for Peter, it's not imagining. And when the energy field is quickened, you can run your palm a few inches from your arm and feel the energy hum along your arm. Or hold up your fingers in apposition and in the gap see a creamy luminescence.

It's really something.

Ahhh. What *something*? Is it just a parlor trick? But after all, what are we made of?

Energy! So much more space than solid thingness. The same energy that's in the vivid world around us. Is it so extraordinary we can learn to feel it? A decade ago he perceived it too intensely. Now, older, maybe he can handle it without losing his marbles?

A Hasidic master says:

"If we bring a person who has always lived in darkness suddenly into the open air, he will not be able to withstand the light. Therefore it is necessary to reveal the light gradually, beginning with showing a small crack through which to see only a small bit of light; afterwards, we expand the crack until it is a window, and afterwards we bring a person outside and show them the light."

The air opens, and he breathes in the silence. He doesn't usually ask himself about God; it's simply as if God is present and he, Peter, is breathing God in.

But then, something starts to come through the silence. A music.

That's when he should have stopped.

Over a decade ago, waves of light, too bright; now waves of sound, too intense, a forefinger pressing his breastplate.

Peter Weintraub has recently become aware that the energy is associated with sound as well as light. Music of the spheres? No. A hum in the streets, hum of blood in his ears, the whoosh and hum when you listen to a seashell. Or is it some problem of his middle ear?

Strangely, the sounds seem to grow as someone approaches him, say crossing a street as he crosses in the opposite direction, and to fall away as they pass him, goodbye, goodbye. And increasingly, it takes the shape of language, as if it were almost communicating, as whispered breath, the thoughts of others. Boring enough, these thoughts. But to dissolve boundaries: to slip unnoticed into other souls—that isn't boring at all. Like playing with the dial of a radio, skipping from station to station, blurring between stations, hearing two at the same time. Radio in a distant room. Whispers. Or faint music. The thump in your chest.

Careful. Be careful.

A decade ago the vision had been fearful. At first it had seemed beautiful—a radiance surrounding people, a glow in their faces. What a lovely truth! Ah, so that's who we are! But the glow didn't last. It became painful to look at so much pain. Ah, so this, this is what her life is! This is what his life is! And mine! Not a holy unity: jagged lines of turbulent energy in mutual opposition.

He'd had to smother his awareness if he wanted to keep his job, to hold his life in balance. Since then, for ten years, the awareness has been kept at bay. He opens his heart to his wife, to his children. But even to Rachel or to his children—grown now, married, with young children of their own—he doesn't speak about it. Finally, by covering up, he was so fully accepted again at his work—a software firm in downtown Boston—that he was put in charge of new product development as vice-president.

They enjoy him at work, he knows, although—no, not *although*, it's *because*—they think him a maverick. They like it that in his office behind a half-open door, he waves his hands to conduct music that only he hears. It used to be over headphones. Now it's ear buds linked to a smart phone in his pocket. His freedom makes them feel free. Even McAndrews, Bruce McAndrews, CEO, grins at him as they pass in the hall, as if they shared some comic secret. But Peter has guarded himself against the vision: those lines of energy. Better not to know so much about other people, about himself.

Gradually, the music he's hearing—not the Mahler or Vaughan-Williams over ear buds but the secret music, another form of the same energy—is threatening. As if he has a new sense, as if he can hear a wavelength other people can't, as a dog can hear a pitch beyond human hearing. Peel open the crack and the world hidden inside the world will come flooding in. The voices blur one into the other, each in a different key. A dissonant music, tone against adjacent tone. Like the tritone, forbidden by the Church in the Middle Ages as demonic, the "devil's triad."

Oh, sure, there's sex in the mix, songs or hints of songs of longing, of love, and the sad songs of damaged souls, incomplete souls hungry for money or respect or meaning. But—maybe it's his receiving set?—mostly he hears on the street, in the office, a music of pain: *worry* in counterpoint with grief and rage. A house in foreclosure, a wife with a cancer devouring her, a dying child.

I'm making too much of this—just the way I did before. Fool! Is it music, is it even sound? Music, if at all, in a distant room, at the very edge of hearing. Waves of air, almost visible. If music, does it mean anything? Not willing to take a chance this time, he calls for an appointment. "Dr. Ackerman," he says over the phone, "I'm afraid I may be at the edge of another 'psychotic episode'" — language that by its distancing, by the implied quotation marks around it, reassures the doctor he's really okay, *not* at the edge of psychosis: words that falsify his experience.

Because once you've been there you can't help but know.

"Last time, I believe, I prescribed an anti-anxiety medication."

"Maybe I'll need something stronger."

For there's an enemy inside him. He has to lock the creature up.

He stops practicing *chi gung*. He's afraid it feeds the creature.

"What's wrong? What's happening to you?" Rachel asks. "You look upset." She helps him with his trench coat. When she's nervous she talks fast, erratically. "Do you know, these last few weeks you've been acting very strangely. I've even wondered — well, I've wondered if you're seeing someone. That's nonsense, I know, isn't that nonsense? But, Peter, you seem so preoccupied. You seem to be floating in your own world."

"Me? '*Seeing* someone,'" he laughs. "Oh, Rachel! I'm almost sixty years old. My doctor — that's who I'm seeing."

"Your doctor? Dr. Ackerman? What's wrong? Are you sick and not telling me? You're not, are you?"

"No. No. I'm kidding. Just a check-up. 'Seeing someone,'" he laughs again. "Don't you know better than that?"

"Of course. I do. I was half kidding. But you don't know how strange you've been."

"Have I been? Ah! I'm your man of mystery."

"Oh, stop." Rachel shuts her eyes a moment as if to remember his strangeness. She sighs.

She's brought home a cloth bag full of groceries. It sits on the kitchen table between them. He sees or feels or hears her glow, a rush of music, its harmony. What a sweet comfort to live with Rachel. Except once in awhile when it's not. Congratulations, he says to himself without irony, for having married her all those years ago. Coming from a damaged family like his! What a smart guy you are. You should win an award for marrying the right woman. Mazel tov! "Seeing someone," indeed!

He feels the exact moment she's about to unpack groceries; they reach together into the bag. Hands dance as they reach in and put things away, reach in and put things away.

He's picked up his prescription but puts the pills in the medicine cabinet, sticks them behind other pills so Rachel doesn't notice and say, *What are these?* For he's not willing to blur away, give up, this awareness.

Now, walking through the aisles of a Home Depot, he

keeps hearing the Truth, or what he thinks of as The Truth. It's as if he can hear something deeper than thought, as if he knows more than do the souls he's tuning into. He's listening to something they emanate but can't hear. It's not just the words going through their heads; it's an invisible radio, faint, the frequency faintly audible, visible, as waves of energy.

Very unnerving—especially at the yearly party, a late spring party—that the company CEO, McAndrews, is throwing for friends. Are they *friends*, he and Bruce McAndrews? They've been friends and not quite friends for almost thirty years.

On the brief drive to Newton Peter grows silent. He's worried. Handing the keys to one of the black-shirted men parking cars, walking the brick path with Rachel and a carload of other guests, he sees he shouldn't have come. He's not ready for the noise and confusion, cacophony of souls whispering under the laughter and blabber.

Bruce McAndrews slaps him on the shoulder and pretends to flirt with Rachel. Then he's off to welcome other guests.

A guitarist is playing Piazzolla. About thirty, forty people stand around in clumps, chatting. More keep coming. Peter is often quiet at a party but it's worse tonight. He stays remote. Tonight the voices under the voices frighten him. It's hard to pretend to believe in the selves the guests are trying to sell each other.

Oh, we're having such a good time. Oh, it's so pleasant to see you again! We're telling funny stories about each other, we're remembering travels in Provence or Tuscany.

Rachel is on his arm. "Get me a drink?"

"Sure, sure. You bet. Coming right up." *Smile.* He smiles into her eyes to reassure her and sees her looking back with concern. The bar takes up a corner of the large room. There are bottles of very good wine, of expensive single-malt scotch, of fine bourbon. He gets doubles of bourbon for them, and the drink helps him. Helps her.

He knows she's worried for him.

We're so delighted to see you. I've forgotten — where does your son go to college? No! Really! Perhaps he knows . . .

Peter tries to listen only to these ordinary conversations, hear what people want him to hear. Still, he can't block the whisperings underneath.

I'm not important to him.

That one is such a little slut.

I want to kill that big shot sonofabitch.

Other whispers are even more disturbing.

I'm going to take that bastard for all he's worth.

I don't love her, I've never loved her.

What does it mean to die? Next year I won't be at a party, I'll be dead. What's "dead"? There'll be a body in a grave. This skin. Where will "I" be? The "I" won't be. My children will speak at my funeral. Stop this. Stop.

Dying. Who's dying here? He doesn't know. Everyone, of course—but who's dying soon? He wants to avoid knowing. Yet he can't help scanning the room—smiling faces at a pleasant party. So much laughter. One couple dances a tango—or, really, camps the tango, the woman kicking up the heels of her high-heeled shoes. In broken air, he feels waves of an erotic pulse in the room.

Deb McAndrews comes over to talk to Rachel; she takes her aside, and Peter goes back to the bar for a ginger ale. Bruce McAndrews is getting sloshed: he tosses one back, has his glass filled again. "What's this about goddamn ginger ale?" he says to Peter.

"I already had a double. I'm driving."

"You're a snob, Pete," he laughs. "You know that? You pretend you're a free soul but you're one big s. n. o. b. "

"Maybe."

"No maybe about it. Maybe this, maybe that. That's you."

Maybe because Bruce McAndrews is drunk, maybe because he's standing right here, Peter is flooded by his unique energy. Peter says, very quietly, "It's *you*—you're real sick? Bruce?"

"I've got pancreatic cancer. Is that a sonofabitch? How the hell did you know?"

"I didn't exactly."

"Who told you? Do I look that bad?"

"You look great. I'm really sorry, Bruce."

"You're not a snob. I was just pulling your chain. I'll tell you, 'cause I'm a little smashed, I like working with you. I always have. You're a good guy. You make it come alive."

"I like working with you, too. So. They're going to give you radiation?"

"Jesus. I don't want to talk about it." He puts a forefinger to his lips.

"Anything you need from me, man, just say so."

"Yeah, yeah. Okay. Here's what I need. Don't make a big deal, don't tell anybody. Not a goddamn soul. Tell me — does everybody know?"

"No idea."

"How did you know?"

"I don't know how. I mean it."

"Come *on*."

Deb and Rachel are heading over, threading their way through the crowd. No more time to talk. Peter grabs Bruce around the shoulder and hugs — hugs hard. Kisses his cheek — smooth, recently shaven, smelling of cologne. Out of embarrassment or as a cover, Bruce starts guffawing. He waves at someone across the room, and he's gone.

The music is full of darkness. Peter tries to listen instead to the guitarist's music.

He doesn't speak on the drive home. He finds himself weeping, blowing his nose, already mourning, and has to pull over and let Rachel drive.

"What is it, honey? I know. It's Bruce, isn't it? Deb told me."

Why, he wonders, should he be the one to perceive the truth? But hasn't it always been there? As a child, didn't he know that under the surface, painfully, a real life was going on?

He'd try to comfort his mother or calm his father. *What do you mean?* she'd say. *Me? I'm a happy wife and mother.* Then middle of the night he'd wake to see her standing by the door to his bedroom, smoking, holding an ash tray, rocking and talking to herself. Or he'd wake to hear them fighting again, screaming in whispers, stage whispers, *You sonofabitch, oh, you sonofabitch.* And he, *What do you do for me?* And she, *I'm not your toilet, mister.*

A happy wife and mother, she'd assure him the next afternoon.

Ahh, every family has its ups and downs, his father would say.

But then there were times the fury would break from his father. He'd slam his big fist into walls. Peter would lock his door and his father would thump and thump until its panels cracked. He didn't want to actually break in — he could have easily. And she — she'd pick up a kitchen knife and go for his father, then stop and stare at the knife as if it were a wondrous object, as if she were acting in a Shakespearean tragedy, turn the knife toward herself and say, *Hmm,* and his father would grab it away — as, of course, he was meant to — and slap her — delicately — into "sense." Her eyes would roll as if she were gaga. Or she'd throw dishes. No, not *throw.* She'd politely *drop* a dish and watch it crack, then say, *Come on. Shall I break some more? Let's have some fun. What do you say, big boy?*

But it's not that rage was the truth and pleasantries were the veneer. He knew the rage was as false as the denial. It was high drama—*her* drama—and ultimately, Peter thinks, his father took it up, learned it from her. She closed the windows so the neighbors wouldn't hear; he followed her and opened them. Under the drama was his father's fear and hatred of his son. Well, he had reasons. For she'd made Peter contemptuous of his father, she'd used him to get at this man who'd obliterated her fantasy of becoming a grand New York matron.

All that madness, those poor damaged souls. *My own damaged soul.* The terrible drama acted-out something in himself. He was excited to be part of the drama, sipping its energy, but able to stand back just a little. It was a school for teaching him to read the truth. So that when, in middle age, the air first opened and he *saw* and *heard*, it was just a different form of what he'd always known:

There's a dangerous, dark, exciting world under the world they sell you.

As soon as he remembers his mother and father, remembers the life of that house, he starts imagining he sees them, though they're long dead. Taking the T to work, he sees, past the bodies, past the briefcases and backpacks of other commuters, his father, his hand raised, holding onto a nickel-plated overhead bar—sees him just for a moment, then realizes he's created him, the way you might turn a pile of clothes into a large dog. Only for a moment. *I'm not crazy yet.* It's someone else, or it's no one; a quick glance tricked him, that's all.

And then his mother, as he turns a corner near Faneuil Hall. No, no. Just someone who walks like his mother, holds her head high like his mother. Her amused, theatrical pose. *I shall return in a moment,* she'd say in her throaty voice, the accent stage-British though her first language was Yiddish. *I shall return more poignant than ever.* Here's simply someone on her way to work, no ghost. Still, he hurries after her. She's gone.

There again, there she is. Her reflection in a glass shop door. And now the voices start.

He wants to blot them out. Blot out the memory of his mother, his father, not see the dead as living; not see living people as the dead. But they keep appearing. He's awake but the dreams keep coming. Like seeing the stars in daytime. They're there, always there, but invisible against the ambient light. The surface of consciousness is like sunlight, keeping dreams invisible. But he sees; out of the corner of his eye, there they are. They're dream fragments, not ghosts. He knows that.

Are you seeing someone? Rachel asked. *Well, as a matter of fact, I am: my poor, dead mother.* And let's face it: he's hungry to see his mother and even his father. Though he knows he's making them up. Oh, not to see the enraged tragedians of his childhood; it's his mother and father the way they were as old people, softer, so much softer, actually kind to each other. The old scripts discarded.

After his father died, his mother loved to sigh and say, *We may have had our differences, your father and I, but we had such a very good marriage.*

He's stashed a few pills, Dr. Ackerman's pills, in a tiny plastic bag in his wallet. He touches the bag but no, he holds off. He has an important meeting this afternoon; he doesn't want to be a zombie.

He takes the elevator up to the company offices. He stops in front of Jeanine Stafford's desk. "I see Bruce for a minute?" Jeanine protects her boss like a tiger. But today she says, "I'll tell him you're here, Mr. Weintraub. He asked to see you when you got in."

Bruce McAndrews looks up from his computer. "Well, I kind of spilled the beans Saturday night."

"It'll go no further. I promise."

"I still haven't figured out who told you. But never mind. I was touched. You *cared,* for Christsake."

"Anything you need, Bruce, we'll treat it as run of the mill reorganization."

"They'll know soon enough. Jesus."

"Nobody will know. Not yet. You look good." He's not exactly lying, but he's not telling Bruce about the pallor of his skin, the deep bags under his eyes.

"I know I can rely on you, buddy."

Can he? If Bruce knew what a peculiar customer I am . . . . But strangely, when he's at work, he feels almost normal.

At work he barely hears the almost-music, barely sees the air open to the throb of energy.

He does his job. In fact, he's enlarged his job; he's been helping grow the company. Selling big time their new software, promoting a new website. Now maybe Bruce will want to sell the company. He's never wanted that, but now he might. With the stock and stock options they've got, they'd all be in great shape.

At once a pang goes through Peter: without the company to keep him stable, what will happen to him?

After the three o'clock meeting he prepares an email for clients, talks to their web designer, makes a few calls. So that it's well into rush hour before he gets away. Workers, tired, end of a long day, are flooding from office buildings, pouring out of City Hall onto the broad, red brick plaza, down the steps to the T. And suddenly, there's the music of pain. And maybe because of Bruce McAndrews, because the dying and the dead are on his mind, Peter sees all the people in the plaza in the process of dying: skull beneath the skin. He imagines these faces dissolving, all the differentia of life dissolving. We're not talking hallucinations here. More fragments of dream in daylight. The opening of the T stop is a mouth in the earth swallowing the living.

Is death always the underlying music?

He shuts his eyes. Opening them, he looks in his wallet again for the little plastic bag with the pills. He remembers from a decade ago: they don't work instantly, but if he takes one, soon he'll feel a mild buzz, and the promise of relief will itself be enough to give him relief. But then he'll shut down as dream maker. The world will just *be* — be without meaning. Dream figures will dissolve, music will fade. There'll be no more whispers.

He puts away the pills, puts away the wallet.

Home, he finds Rachel sitting in the living room with a drink and a book. A Schubert sonata plays through their new speakers. Well, thank God. For *this* music he's grateful.

He squirrels in next to Rachel. On the end table, a pile of papers for her to correct. She has a wine glass ready for him — the bottle, chilled, sits in a terracotta cooler. He pours himself a glass of white wine.

"How was your day?" she asks.

"I talked to Bruce this morning. He's keeping it a secret."

"I've been thinking of him a lot. Is it okay if we go out to dinner with them . . ."

" — I think so," he says. "Yes. Or have them here."

". . . And really talk? I'll call Deb. It's not good for him to keep it so hidden."

"Not good," Peter says, taking that in, knowing that he himself has been keeping his deepest life a secret, even from Rachel. Which is a loss. A loss, he knows. It's even a kind of betrayal. For there's less of him to meet her. The deepest stuff is covered over. But what if he tells her? Won't she think he's gone off the deep end? Well? And hasn't he? But in quiet, reasonable tone he says, "But maybe he needs to hold it in. Maybe that's not bad—to know but not to say."

They're silent for a moment. "Sounds like you have something to say," she says.

He says, quietly and precisely: "Listen. Rachel. I'd tell you if I could. I don't know how to tell you. There's a world under the world. Everything is connected. As if what we see is an encoding of that deeper world."

"*What?*"

"See? Not possible to tell you. I said 'everything is connected.' It's what we say in prayers, right?—*Adonoy echad*—God is one, is Oneness, there's nothing not-God. God's the spider spinning a web, but He's also the web. All right. Try this, Rachel. Breathe and be silent with me. Feel what happens."

"What do you mean, honey?"

"Be silent. You'll begin to feel the deeper world come into you, like music or breath."

"You're serious?"

"Don't worry. I'm talking metaphor." He sighs. "I'm hoping I can handle it this time."

"Handle? Handle what, exactly?" She's worried for him. The worry will keep her from hearing the music. So, keeping it light, he tells her about playing with a ball of *chi*. "It's really simple," he says. "Try it. It's really something."

"Oh, you've told me about your ball of *chi*. That's never worked for me."

"Well, it's not all that important," he says. "Tell me about school."

Bruce is dying, under hospice care at home. Like a dying king, he receives friends and family when he's up to it. No business calls. None. He's lucky not to have bad side effects from the morphine. "Fabulous drug, morphine," he slurs, "absolutely terrific—when it doesn't leave me a zombie. Mellow, man. So mellow I love every son of a bitch around. And I don't have to worry," he laughs, "about becoming an addict. There won't be time." He keeps it light, Bruce, so Peter smiles, listens. Long silences between sentences—even between words. Bruce isn't aware of the gaps. But in the gaps, Peter hears a distant conversation. Far off, far off. What's being said? He knows, we all know. We don't want to know that we know.

The rented hospital bed in the paneled library lets Bruce sit up. "This is like receiving mourners at my own funeral. Not bad." Then he gets serious. "Tough on Deb. Tough. Be good to Deb, you and Rachel, or I'll haunt you. Okay? Kids'll leave, she'll be alone except for friends."

"We'll be good friends to her."

"I know, Pete. Course."

"*Pete?* Since when am I *Pete*?" Peter laughs. "Thirty years and all of a sudden I'm *Pete*."

"In my condition, Pete, I'm allowed all kinds of leeway. Christ, I gotta get something out of this."

Following Deb's instructions, Peter spends just fifteen minutes with Bruce. Next day Rachel stops in, hugs
Bruce, spends a little time with Deb.

Heat of the summer, but cool still this morning. Even
cooler in the small sanctuary for the Tuesday morning
minyan. Sun already high through the clearstory windows—you can't sit on one side of the little room or the
sun shines right in your eyes. The service begins with
blessings of gratitude—for the body and for the soul, for
being free, for being made in the image of God.

Gratitude blesses the one offering blessing. The
rhythmic verses offer comfort.

Taking part in the minyan especially moves Peter
today. Sam Schulman, facing the ark with Torah scroll
inside, chants the morning prayers. Some members of the
minyan murmur along, some read to themselves, Hebrew
or English, moving their lips. A complicated fugue of
whisper and chant, rhymed, ancient music, in rhythm to
which he rocks, eyes shut. When they pray the Standing
Prayer, Peter names Bruce in the blessing for the sick. He
doesn't ask for healing but for peace, strength, comfort.
Miracles he doesn't expect. But if we're all part of the
One, he thinks, then isn't that the miracle? We all take
part in the music. How can we ever die? Flesh becomes
grass; our children are flesh of our flesh . . . . Don't we live
in those we've touched? Here's the point of the prayers:

we're held by the web, the Unity of which we're a part.
No. No — we *are* the web.

He's praying on automatic. In the middle of a prayer,
thinking these comforting thoughts, he blurts a laugh.
Guffaw! Heads turn. *Oh,* they think, *it's just Peter.*

What malarkey, he says to himself. Not untrue, but
emotional morphine. Folks, Peter says as if addressing a
throng, or addressing at least the other congregants, the
sad news is, we really do die. The music under the music,
that's what it tells us. "No man is an island," Donne says.
"Any man's death diminishes me." Maybe not any man,
but Bruce — his death will diminish Peter, while at the
same time, yes, Bruce will reside, reside partly, in Rachel
and Peter, in Deb, in their children. So the music will go
on and on. Peter can't help but hear it. He can't help but
hum, silently, along.

* * *

The Embezzler

and the Rabbi

RABBI ARI STEIN looks like the subject of a portrait by Jan Steen or Franz Hals. Broad-faced, ruddy and plump, mid-forties, curly black hair, he'd be perfect with a tankard of beer and a long white meerschaum pipe. His belly, rounded but hard, not flabby, goes ahead of him through the world. He's physically powerful. Sam Schulman has seen him lift — lift easily — a hundred pound box of prayer books.

He's easygoing, Ari, "flexible" — a word he says often, *flexible* — not *doctrinaire* — yet he's able to carry the huge load of a rabbi — leading services, preparing *divrei Torah* — words of Torah — for a Saturday morning service, presiding at a funeral, leading a discussion, planning and finding support for a capital campaign and for the synagogue's little vegetable garden, it goes on and on. What doesn't a rabbi have to do?

Ari is quietly proud that at a time when young rabbis were having a hard time finding congregational positions, he was snatched, right out of seminary, to become rabbi of B'nai Shalom, a mid-sized congregation in Brookline, Mass. His wife Lori, a psychiatrist, was delighted—she had contacts in the Boston area, old friends who could help her build a practice. Ari believes, not flattering himself but not exhibiting false modesty, that the congregation feels lucky to have found him. He's thought of as *soft*, but he's liked and respected. He finds pleasure in parsing out the arguments in the Talmud—he studies with Sam Schulman, Gershom Samuels, Alex Koenigsberg a page of Talmud nearly every Friday. After six years many congregants have become friends. He and Lori are close to a number of families, especially those whose children are the age of his own—Aaron now eleven, Sarah eight.

But a few days ago—Friday—everything turned terribly upside down. Larry Klein, Board Treasurer, knocked on his office door looking ragged. "We have to talk." Since then, they've spent days and nights going over the books for the past five years. Stopping only for Shabbat, they went from suspicion to certainty. Monday Ari called the fraud unit of the Brookline Police Department and Ben Adler, the lawyer who does pro bono work for B'nai Shalom. His third call was to Nick Shorr, the synagogue's Executive Director. "Please be in my office at two tomorrow afternoon."

Tuesday morning, on little sleep, weighed down by what he's discovered, worried about the upcoming meeting with Shorr, Ari looks for Sam Schulman in the small sanctuary. Sam's putting away prayer books used in the

morning minyan. "Sam? Can we talk a few minutes?"
They sit in the rabbi's office, Ari and Sam. "Sam?
We've been robbed."

"Robbed? Someone broke in?"

"*Embezzlement.*"

The one word, like a curse, lips breaking up the word
into syllables. Silence. Now Ari lifts a heavy breath of air
into his lungs. "It's been going on for five years. Larry
Klein finally spotted something peculiar and called me.
We spent two nights sitting with the books, Larry and
me, totaling it up. We'll need an outside accountant to get
close to the full picture. You're chair of the exec, so I'm
letting you know. But that's not it. You've been a friend. I
need to talk it through, Sam."

Sam waits. Ari collects himself.

"It's well over *two hundred thousand*," Ari says slowly.
"It increased every year. And he called himself a *friend*."
He wraps himself in his arms and rocks, a mourner.

Sam nods. "And this *friend*—we're talking about
someone who has the power to sign checks and take in rev-
enue?" A bitter laugh. "We're speaking of the Executive
Director? Not my favorite person—Nick Shorr."

Rabbi Ari nods. "He kind of pushed a friendship on
me. Maybe he did that to blindside me—it's hard to look
over a *friend's* shoulder. Some friend! Lori is sick about it.
We had them over for dinner, Nick and Nancy, how many
times? We were at his house how many times? Sam, we
went on a week's vacation together!"

They sit, both of them, with one elbow on the arm of a chair, chin cupped in the palm of the hand. A call comes in; Rabbi Stein lets it go to voice mail. He feels soothed by Sam's calm.

"You've called the police?"

"Oh, yes. As soon as we were sure. There's a detective already assigned. It makes me sick. I feel ashamed — to be conned like this."

"And Shorr says . . . ?"

"I haven't spoken to him. I'll confront him this afternoon. You know — I'm actually frightened. As if I were the guilty one. Well. In a way I am."

"It's the board that's responsible."

"I should have been more watchful."

Sam doesn't argue. "What about restitution?" he asks. "How much of what he stole can we get back?"

"You know as much as I do. We both know what a spender he is. In mind's eye," Ari says, shutting his outward eyes, "I see him stepping out of his Lexus SUV or that red MG convertible of his, or strutting down the hall in a beautiful suit or designer jeans and a silk shirt. We should have figured something was wrong. On his synagogue salary?"

"I thought it was Nancy," Sam says, "I thought she must have a trust fund."

Sam looks at his watch. Ari remembers it's a teaching day for Sam. But as they stand, Ari says, "I've been thinking, how can *good* come of this? Of what value is our tradition if, the first time we face evil up close, we feel defeated by it? This can be a time of learning for our congregation. It's a spiritual issue—or I'm in the wrong profession."

Leaving, Sam squeezes Ari's shoulder. "I get what you're going through. Call me anytime you want to talk. Call me. Even middle of the night."

Without Sam there, Ari feels more shaky. He rests. He remembers Nick laughing. He laughs loudly. He tells jokes and laughs at his own jokes.

Nick Shorr came to B'nai Shalom from Jewish Theological Seminary, where he took a degree in Jewish Studies and Public Administration. After JTS, Shorr is said to have "worked wonders" at a synagogue in Cleveland. The board was impressed by his credentials and letters of recommendation.

We envied his ease and his certitude. A can-do person. All that bravura, Ari thinks. *Didn't I know that underneath the arrogant charm Nick was weak? Yet we gave him temptation and opportunity, not checking as long as the books looked correct.*

As he opens his laptop and begins to draft a letter to the community for the board to approve, he imagines with his inner eye another well-dressed man, a man with big beak and long wavy hair fringing a balding pate—it's Bernie Madoff. Why out of all the betrayers in history is he seeing Madoff? Of course: Madoff is Jewish. Most of the people he ripped off were Jews. We expect, from our own, faithfulness, trustworthiness, righteousness. And we say, it's a *shande*, a shame, for the goyim. When someone of the dominant culture does something slimy, the shame is on his own head; when he's a Jew, all Jews are shamed.

Ten years ago while still in his rabbinical program, Ari took a week-long workshop on the "business of synagogues." Financial planning, capital campaigns, budgets. Parenthetically, the danger of financial mismanagement — including embezzlement. *Watch like a hawk?* the workshop leader said. *Yes, but again like a hawk,* he said, *see from a distance. Make sure you don't micromanage. It doesn't behoove a rabbi to be constantly suspicious. But . . . when there's money around you do have to keep your eyes open.*

Yet not to live in a trusting spirit is to lock the heart in a cell without windows. *Pirke Avot* says, *Judge every man on the side of merit.*

And if you trust, others will be trustworthy.

Well. Usually. So he believes.

Most members of the congregation are, he's sure, honest in business dealings. Most, he believes, if they found a thousand dollars in the street, a roll of untraceable bills, would do their best to find the owner. Honesty in business is not a merely ethical injunction; it's an aspect of holiness. In the Talmud we're told: The very first question we will be asked after our death is, "Did you conduct your business affairs with honesty and with probity?"

Ari goes to the synagogue's administrative office. Arlene knows what's going on. She was there Friday morning when he and Larry Klein, Board Treasurer, pulled the books, canceled credit cards, spoke to the bank. Now Ari asks her to put together a file: everything they have on Nick. "And then put me in contact with the rabbi in Cleveland."

She's already made the file; she hands it to him.

The rabbi goes back to his office and calls the Jewish Theological Seminary, then the rabbi in Cleveland. Call leads to call leads to call; the problem is even deeper than he thought. Not only has Nick stolen almost a quarter of a million dollars from B'nai Shalom. His references for the job were fake—fake in Cleveland, fake at JTS. He worked at, but was never administrator of, a synagogue. And he never took a degree at JTS.

At two o'clock sharp Nick comes to the Rabbi's office dressed in a suit. Pin-striped, deep gray, almost black: *I'm a serious man. Let's get down to business.* But he's wearing a broad, "winning" smile, a smile his parents must have taught when they took pictures. Ari is sure Nick's parents took lots of pictures of their charming son. Unsmiling, Ari waves Nick to a seat. Nick is long-legged, lean, a head taller than Ari— a model in a Men's Fashion section of the *Times*. Nick sticks a hand out into the space between them; Ari looks at the hand, lets it hang there in mid-air.

"So what's this about?" Nick asks.

"'About' a quarter of a million dollars. That's what it's about."

Nick laughs. "No. Really."

"You tell me. How much do *you* think you stole from us?"

Nick Shorr just sits, silent, preparing his lines.

"Nick?"

"Am I under review?"

Ari sees a flash of contempt in Nick's eyes. Ari stays silent, sits implacably across the desk. Suddenly he sees Nick is in tears. Ari didn't expect him to break down so soon.

"It started," Nick says, "as a small thing—a few hundred. Once you begin, well, it's hard to stop. You see?" He takes a Kleenex off Ari's desk, meant for a suffering wife, a man mourning a dead father. "I'm deeply sorry, Ari. I'm so, so sorry."

"Go on."

"When I saw how easy it was, I kind of juggled credit cards, I made up imaginary expenses."

"Don't forget—you sent checks to an imaginary company at a post office box."

"That, too. That, too."

Ari keeps his face like stone. "We need to talk about restitution."

Nick Shorr sighs. "Ari! You can't imagine how terrible—"

"—you feel," Rabbi Ari finishes. "I know. You're a

big feeler." He sighs — parody of a sigh — indicating Nick is posturing, playing the role of sufferer. *Let's cut through the bullshit.* Yet, at the same time, he's sighing for the *real* suffering Nick is going through — and doesn't *know* he's going through. Underneath the theatrics, he's sure, lies real suffering.

"Terrible," Nick says. "Terrible. When you called, something in your voice, I knew. I could hardly eat dinner last night. I had to pop a couple of Valium to get to sleep. I've been thinking a lot about this, Ari. How did it start? Oh, I take full responsibility. Full responsibility . . ." He thumps his sternum like a Jew reciting the *Al Chet* prayer, confessing sins on Yom Kippur. But then he adds, lifting a forefinger like a candle ". . . even though . . . I have to say . . . it's not entirely my fault."

"Whose fault, then?"

"Partly Nancy's. Yes! That sounds strange, I know."

"Nancy!"

"Well, yes, actually, yes, in the sense that she pouted, she nagged, she felt entitled — I should bring more money home. For buying decent furniture, for redoing the kitchen. For travel. A Jewish-American princess. Yes! Yes! You don't believe that? And another thing: now, this is explanation, not excuse" — He leans forward so that he's only inches from Rabbi Ari — "I was underpaid, Ari. The synagogue underpaid me. Haven't you yourself apologized to me for not paying me more? So. Listen. Here's the thing. You tell me if this will work."

He hunches forward even more, a quarterback spinning a play. "Suppose you decide to call what I took a *yearly bonus*. Money I *should* have received. See what I mean? I'm asking you to reconfigure the situation. See it this way: *Nick gave himself a bonus to which he was morally entitled.* Help the board see it this way. Okay? So I paid myself an extra $35,000, $40,000, a year. So what?" He holds out his hands, palms up. *Be reasonable.* "It's what I *deserved*! If you're willing, we can finagle with the board a little so we both come out smelling clean. We can make it all go away, Ari. All go away. Think how much better off B'nai Shalom would be."

Ari rolls his desk chair back and laughs. "*Bonuses*! You're some comedian." As Ari takes up the folder, over the corner of its plastic cover he sees anger and contempt in this "friend's" eyes. Ari remembers a phrase he heard somewhere: *A man who is either at your feet . . . or at your throat.*

Amazing the way Nick's face seems to change in the blink of an eye — as his tactics change. First, his brow is furrowed with grief lines, poor fellow, poor fellow, then his jaw tightens, his face hard as metal sculpture. "Tell me," Ari says, "are you in your right mind, Nick? I've investigated — as we should have five years ago. You were *never* Executive Director in Cleveland. You *never* got a degree. You were at JTS one semester."

"You see?" Nick says, lifting a forefinger, as if Ari needed his teaching. "You admit you didn't sufficiently check on me! You weren't careful. You were lazy. That makes you partly responsible. What will the board say about that? Of course the board was lazy too."

Ari is amazed at this chutzpah! What nerve! Like a wife beater who blames his wife for buying him the belt he hits her with. "So I'm guilty for trusting, for not figuring out that you're a con man?" The rabbi speaks in anger — but along with anger, he feels a recognition of Nick's acuteness: *He takes the measure of my weakness; he knows how much I blame myself!* As a way of girding himself, Ari points a finger and leans on Deuteronomy: "'*Cursed is the one who leads a blind person astray.*' That was me, Nick. The blind person."

"*Please.* We can both cite Chapter and Verse. *You shall not deal deceitfully or falsely with one another.* Okay. But I did want the best for the synagogue. Can you believe that?"

"'Best for the synagogue'! Think how much better off the synagogue would be if we had that quarter of a million dollars to bring in scholars, to run programs. We're always over-budget. It's weighed on me: going without — or dipping into the rainy-day fund."

"We were friends, you and I! For your birthday, remember, I bought you two volumes of the *Talmud!* That was out of my own money. Tell me: You haven't decided to press charges, have you? That would be astonishingly stupid for the synagogue."

"The board will be meeting tomorrow evening with an attorney present. You'd better get yourself a lawyer — whatever we decide. Today is our last meeting, you and I, without lawyers present."

As if wounded, Nick whines, "I have a right to speak to the board."

"You can speak to the board. But you have no 'rights.' You're no longer employed." Ari reaches into a drawer, hands Shorr an envelope. "Your contract is terminated for cause. Of course we'll sue for restitution."

Nick stands. "Sue! And my lawyer will counter-sue. Read your employee handbook — which it so happens I wrote! Ha-ha! Termination for cause requires a hearing. Ari, as your friend, I'm sorry, but you must see I have to protect myself." Nick reaches out a hand to place it on Ari's shoulder. Ari shrugs it away. There's that look of contempt again — not even hidden. Nick says, "You were such a pushover. You and the board. Sometimes I was embarrassed taking advantage."

"If you come tomorrow," Ari says, "bring your lawyer. That will be your 'hearing.' Maybe your lawyer can help negotiate restitution. Maybe he can keep you out of prison. The board, not me, will have to decide whether to press criminal charges. Of course, the Prosecutor for the Commonwealth of Massachusetts will have final say."

"You sound like such a fink! Listen — Do you really want to send a friend, and haven't I been a friend? — to prison? I know you don't want that — when it was your own carelessness that allowed me to take my . . . bonuses. And Ari . . ." Nick whispers this: "You know what I'll argue if I'm prosecuted? 'Of course he pretends to believe I was a thief and he's pure. He's paying me back for my relationship with his wife!' "

"My wife? What relationship?"

"Don't freak out. Ask Lori. At least she'll acknowledge our *financial* relationship. I'm going to have to sue the board and sue you, Ari—and drag Lori into it." It's as if he feels sorry for Ari. "Ask Lori about her—well—friendship with me. I hate to hurt a friend. But then, we're none of us such good friends now, are we? If I'm put on trial, I'll argue you were in collusion. And we'll sue for defamation and for unlawful termination."

"With your signature on checks to non-existent vendors? Sue, go ahead. What's this about Lori?"

Nick sighs. "Yes, well, I'll have to involve Lori—what happens when I tell the board or a court that Lori's also dipped into the till? You see, Ari, I knew there might come a day like this. I've protected myself. I have receipts. A computer for your use at home?"

"That was approved by the board."

"Did I tell you that? I lied. It *wasn't*. But in court it's your word against mine. After all, it was Lori who actually bought the computer—with a synagogue credit card."

"I never even asked for it. You said I should have it."

"Tell that to the board. There may not be a case against you—but you'll be tainted. Oh, yes, Ari! They'll never see you the same way again. And do be sure to ask Lori."

"What *are* you, really?"

"Isn't it better that we end our relationship without additional damage?" Nick smiles that grandiose smile of his, waves goodbye, backs out of Ari's office.

It's drizzling a little when Ari leaves B'nai Shalom for the brief walk home. He's hoping it'll be more peaceful, being alone, phone off. But he can't get away from words, words, going through his head, or that cocky look when Nick spoke about Lori. He remembers Nick's hostile smile, sees financial spread sheets, silently recites a list of calls he has to make. Looking at himself reflected in the window of a restaurant, at once he sees he's getting plump. Not good, not good. Plump, protected by his umbrella, he looks so uncool! In spite of his unease about the conversation he'll have to go through with Lori, he so much wants to hold her, to rest in her tenderness and belief in him.

Home, up the steps to the porch, cluttered with plastic children's toys from the family downstairs, he enjoys the way the oval glass panel of the door makes the interior a little mysterious, even romantic. He calls out to Lori, "I'm home. What a day."

"I'm in the kitchen."

He takes off his shoes, stows them in the closet, and gives his damp topcoat a shake and hangs it up. It's a relief to be home, though being home carries new tensions. The condo is a floor-through in a beautiful old Brookline house, a hundred years old, restored and turned into three units a few years ago.

Lori's at the stove; she waves without turning, stirs, stirs. Now turns around. And looks at him. "Oh, it's hard on you. I can see it."

He kisses her cheek, still rehearsing. How can he ask a question about Nick's insinuations? Ari has been with Lori since they were undergraduates at Swarthmore, then all through her medical training and psychiatric residency. They've weathered separations for work, exhaustion, growing differences in what being Jewish means. They've grown very close. So he's ashamed of his rehearsing. He can tell her anything, can admit anything, things he wouldn't admit to anyone else.

"The kids home?"

"Aaron's rehearsing a school play," Lori says. "He'll be home in ten minutes. Sara is playing at Leah's. You can pick her up right after dinner, okay?"

He can tell Lori anything—yet there's something he's having a hard time telling. His rehearsing implies a lack of trust. It's so hard to say: *Nick insinuated he was your lover.* No. What's hard to say is that it's hard to say.

When she asks, "So? Did you see him?" he finds himself crafting his answer, just as if he weren't sure about her. The very delay—he lifts his hand and says, "Please, let's sit down and have some wine"—is shameful.

Finally, he says, "I saw him. He didn't bother to deny. Oh, Lori, the money, the money—what the synagogue could have done with that money. It makes me sick. There's more. Director at that synagogue in Cleveland? No, never.

Graduated from JTS? In a pig's eye. The pathetic liar! In a few minutes time he went from groaning about his guilt to declaring he was entitled to the money as bonuses!"

"Bonuses?"

"And he says—you won't believe this, Lori—that it's partly my fault. Why?—for not suspecting him! The board has some right to say that—but the thief? Oh. And he'll claim that you and I were in collusion with him. If we press charges, he'll say terrible things no one will believe—but they will besmirch us. I guess you'd call it blackmail. Or extortion? For we've done nothing wrong."

"That's pathetic. He *is* a sick man."

"Yes. Exactly. It's my job to feel compassion. That's hard. I feel myself tightening."

"Oh, Ari. There are times tightening is called for." Lori takes an open bottle of wine from the fridge, leads Ari to the living room couch, pats the cushion so he'll sit with her.

He sighs a great sigh and tells her. "Remember when you went to the Apple store to get my laptop? And you used a synagogue credit card? Well, he'd told us the board had approved, but the board never approved. Nor was asked. Nor knew."

He scans the pile of books on the coffee table. *It has to be said.* "There's more. He insinuates that you and he had a personal connection—as lovers. 'Poor Lori—what will exposure do to *her*? What's going to happen to Lori?'"

"Lovers! We were never anything like lovers," she says.

"Of course not. Don't you think I know that?"

"Why did you become his friend in the first place? I never really liked him. He was too smooth."

Ari nods and thinks, nods and thinks. "I sensed a weakness in Nick. I thought I could help him. I got tripped up by my own compassion. And—well, he does have a kind of charm."

"Exactly. Charm. He has charm all right. That's what put me off right away."

"And he knows a lot about a lot of different things. Remember the last time he came over?" Ari counts on his fingers: "He talked about J. S. Bach as a father, Catherine the Great as an administrator. Let's see . . . and Sabbatai Zevi at the Turkish sultan's court—and the harmonic innovations of—wasn't it?—Stravinsky. He's really something."

"Purchasing that computer—I was so pleased they were giving it to you. They should. It's for professional work. Anyway, that was all I had to do with him."

"Of course."

"But," she says, "I suppose he could make insinuations."

Instantly Ari's breath comes quick and hot. "Oh? How?"

"I didn't know whether to tell you this, Ari. Almost every time he and Nancy came for dinner, and on that vacation we took together, he'd find a time he and I were alone, say in the kitchen, and half kidding, half serious, he'd paw me a little, try to kiss me, or *pretend* to try to kiss me. He'd say, 'Doctor, Doctor, what's wrong with me? Could it be love, Doc?' At first I thought it was a joke. Then I realized it was no joke; the joke was his cover. He was after me. He'd call when you were out and want to meet. Last time he and Nancy were here, I told him if he bothered me again, I'd tell you. And I made an interpretation he wasn't ready for—I wouldn't have made it early in therapy if he were my patient. I suggested it was really *you*, Ari, he was after. Oh! He got so angry and cold. Then he backed away and said, 'When I want your services as psychiatrist I'll pay for them.'"

"You should have told me."

"I know. I know."

The situation has changed. Any sympathy he felt for a sick man has gone. If Nick were present, he'd punch out the bastard. But he can't let Lori see what he's feeling! On the surface he stays calm. He says to himself, again and again, a mantra to help himself calm down, a passage from Leviticus: *You shall not take vengeance or bear a grudge.* All he says is, "Nick does need therapy."

"Yes. But therapy rarely helps," Lori says, "in a case like his. The patient puts up a false self, another false self over the false self. You think you've got down to his damaged soul—and find you haven't touched it. You're interacting with another false self."

"Lying lips are an abomination to the Lord," he recites. "That's true, Lori—but it's not that a transcendent Judge will grow angry. It's damage done to the soul of the one with lying lips. You're cut off from your own true life and from others. The mask becomes a prison."

Lori reaches over and massages Ari's neck. "I know. And to be betrayed by someone you gave your friendship . . . ."

"When he first came for an interview there was something about him made me feel funny. But on paper he looked great. And he's so precise, so decisive—not *my* best qualities, I know. I didn't pay attention to my feelings."

"Your 'best qualities,'" Lori says. She leans toward him, places her cheek against his. "You're the dearest man—an open-hearted man, compassionate, ethical—an ethical man. But the negative side of open-heartedness can be slackness. Carelessness."

"Ouch! I know, I know!" He laughs, puts up his hands to hide his face: she's holding a clear mirror up before him; he doesn't like what he sees.

"You don't even balance your checkbook. You're great leading kids in a nigun or helping a child prepare for her Bat Mitzvah. You write passionately. You're wonderful at the bedside of a sick person. I love you, my dummy! I love your open heart. But you were overjoyed when Nick came along and you didn't have to look over the figures."

After dinner the children are a respite. He listens to Aaron's lines for the play, then drives to pick up Sarah at Leah's. Leah's mother, one of his congregants, already knows about the embezzlement—he can see it in her eyes—but is kind enough not to bring it up. She simply, wordlessly, gives him a hug. Home, he retreats to his study.

He expects a bad night. He types another draft of his letter on his laptop—he'll never use that laptop without thinking of Shorr—a letter pending approval by the board to tell the community that *synagogue funds have been embezzled, but the synagogue is not to be defined by this theft. We're bigger than that.* He has a nagging feeling that maybe he is not big enough, not spiritually adequate for the profession. He professes—but maybe falsely. Has he been a spiritual leader? Has he helped bring anyone closer to the truth of their lives? Has he helped himself live the truth?

He sits back and begins to laugh at himself for taking himself so seriously.

Calls, emails, all Wednesday. Ari can't keep up. It's his job as rabbi to contain and diffuse the expressions of anger that reach him. He's the dumping grounds even when the congregant is sympathetic, when he, Ari, isn't being attacked. Word has gotten out, and the emails make him wonder: *are* we big enough, healthy enough as a community, to get through this? The emails are so charged with anger, with an appetite for revenge. It's partly the almost thousand dollars a family that's been stolen, of course. To get the community to dig into their pockets again will be tough. But the feeling of vengeful anger — that, he'll have to explore in his Torah talks and "Rabbi's Blog" posts.

Home, he eats a sandwich Lori made for him, walks back to B'nai Shalom — goes to the small sanctuary, sometimes used as a meeting room. He's early. It's summer; the sun hasn't set. Slanting west to east through the clearstory windows, the sunlight makes the room a different place from its look in the morning. The paneling glows. Chairs have been placed in a circle. Most of the fifteen board members are already there, and so is Nick and a man Ari assumes to be his lawyer. Nancy's here, too. Ari goes up to her, sits beside her and takes her hand, pats her hand. She's frozen — scared, angry — angry at everyone, he supposes. Her hand stiff as sculpture. "You're brave coming here," he whispers. "I'm really sorry for what you're going through. Remember: no one's judging *you*."

Nancy's so pretty, so young, fifteen years younger than Ari — maybe more. She works as a dental hygienist. Ari hopes she makes enough to support the family on her own for awhile. Maybe a long while. She has a little girl.

No one is looking at Nick; to remove himself, Nick is looking up at the clearstory windows as if speaking to God. A hum in the room. The members of the board are milling, whispering, or sitting and looking through a stapled sheaf that the synagogue president, Ray Chernov, has distributed — losses the Treasurer, Larry Klein, has come up with so far. Ari glances at Nick. Nick motions with his head, *Can we step outside and talk?*

They pass the last member of the board on her way in as they go out. In the hall Nick speaks quietly, but the sound echoes, so he has to speak slowly. "Ari? I want you to know, I'm not going to mention you, I'm not going to mention Lori. I can't do that to a friend. You've never hurt me. You see how those folks in there want blood? I'd appreciate a good word from you."

A good word! Ari consciously tightens himself against sympathy. "You!" he says. You went after my wife. You went after Lori. Now you want my help?"

"If you must know, making a play for Lori was . . . a tactic. In case I was found out, well, you'd have a hard time confronting me if I were Lori's lover. Okay?"

Ari is stunned. The falseness! That Nick can speak about the attempt to make use of Lori as a *tactic*, as if that made it better! "I'll say nothing to help you. Don't expect any help from me," Ari says and turns away.

They go back inside. There they are, members of the board, friends as well as congregants, people he's worked with on committees — led this one's son's Bar Mitzvah, led that one's father's funeral. Yet now he fears their wrath.

He nods to Ben Adler, synagogue lawyer pro bono, and shakes hands with Ari's lawyer, a small man in a black suit. Now Sam Schulman, as chair, opens the meeting. They meet tonight, Sam begins, in "extraordinary session." He speaks calmly, evenly. "Our wound has been cauterized. But it's still very painful."

Time for Rabbi Ari to stand and offer a blessing, ending, "May we make holy use of the pain: the deception and loss. We have a serious obligation to the whole community to find out what's happened and decide whether to press charges, but our *inner* work is to keep from becoming part of an angry mob. If we're quiet inside, thoughtful, then what we experience as a terrible betrayal can also become an opportunity for spiritual learning."

Some nod, some won't look at him. Is *he* quiet inside? Hardly.

Nick stands. "I'd like to speak. Is that all right?"

"So he can excuse his lying self?" Leon Cole murmurs. A few people laugh.

"No excuse. No excuse," Nick says. "I've been thinking and thinking about what I did. I don't expect to be forgiven because I was weak—weak now and in the past. I've gotten away with a lot. No excuse. Except . . . well, except that I assumed the rabbi knew and was letting me get away with it because I was underpaid. I still don't know if he knew. But I'd like to stay out of prison. I have a family to support. I need to make restitution, and I can't do that if I'm in prison. The Talmud requires restitution. I'm committed to paying the synagogue back. Are my commitments worth anything? I can't see why you'd think so. At least I want to apologize for what I've done." He stands, head hanging, ox ready for the slaughter.

Ari turns over in his mind Nick's words: the subtle smearing of Ari — an apology that's no apology. And the music of Nick's speech, the careful rise and fall of his intonations, false, so false, Mr. Charm, narrator of a TV infomercial. Ari remembers what Lori said: masks under masks under masks.

Ari realizes how much he himself has been wounded. He'll never trust in the same way again. Well — nor should he. Time to grow up. I've been playing the innocent. The young, idealistic rabbi, counting on everyone else to let him remain innocent.

No one but Ari exchanges glances with Nick, who, with Nancy and the lawyer, gathers papers and leaves the room. Now everyone wants to speak at once. The meeting goes on and on, venting, venting. Anger with self-congratulations: "After being victim of such criminal dishonesty," says Nathan Samuels, a founding member of B'nai Shalom, "I feel tempted — after forty years — to drop my membership. But my flight would further hurt a community I love. I'm not going to do that." Members attack one another, voices quivering; they're angry that the meeting is going on so long — yet no one's willing to end it. The sanctuary fills with ugly righteousness. Treasurer Larry Klein is the board's hero, though many ask why it took him so long.

Ari is more and more the object of covert attacks, even more than Nick — though always board members preface their attacks with sympathy: "Rabbi Ari is as much a victim as anyone." Then comes the real point: "I can imagine how terrible the Rabbi feels. How betrayed. I don't believe for a moment that he knew anything. But that's a shame, isn't it? I *can't* understand why he wasn't more on top of things, wasn't able to see what was going on." He's spoken *of*, in third person, as "the Rabbi," not spoken *to*.

Then one woman, Lily Sharken, does speak to him. She's loved for her loud scarves and outrageous speech. "Rabbi dear, it's time somebody told you. You like being sensitive and kind. We love that in you. But don't be too easy on yourself, Rabbi Ari. You must work with the board to oversee the budget. I'm not attacking you. But I'm chastising, *fershtaste?* You're a good man. But it was your job and our job to catch and pounce upon Mr. Shorr's creative manipulation of our budget."

Ari needs to stay above the quarrel; he's grateful to see Sam get up. When Sam stands, he takes up a lot of room; when he speaks, his rich baritone makes people listen. "Here's what I see going on tonight. We're angry. We want to be paid back, want to punish someone who's stolen from us — and grieve that the man we worked with turns out to be so damaged, turns out to be someone we never knew. And we grieve for his wife and child, who will likely suffer the most."

Lots of nods. A committee is formed to meet with Nick's attorney, negotiate terms of restitution, report back with recommendations. Will they press charges? Yes, no question. Now the meeting can break up; everyone goes home. It's dark out. Ari walks along Beacon, past a closed funeral parlor, a closed deli, an open coffee shop, hardly anyone there, and up the hill to home and family.

So damn hard, he thinks, to be a rabbi—a position in which everything has emotional and spiritual meaning. But that's the beauty of it. There are times he's overjoyed, feels blessed: everything matters, nothing is ordinary, or, rather, the ordinary is always charged with meaning. There are times being a rabbi feels like a great privilege— maybe now more than ever.

Then there are times he wishes he were selling shoes.

Months go by. Nancy Shorr has returned to the synagogue $35,000, borrowed from her parents and a trust fund. Nick will do prison time—but by agreeing to a plea bargain and a plan for restitution, he'll have charges reduced; if he goes to prison, he'll be out in a year. At the sentencing Rabbi Ari speaks before the judge: "Mr. Shorr has cooperated with us and has expressed remorse." Then, surprising himself, he adds: "But he's not to be trusted. We've found that his word is worth nothing."

The story dies down. The community comes together. There's sympathy for the Rabbi. Lori invites Nancy Shorr for coffee; Nancy wants nothing to do with them. She's living with her mother in Ipswich. Ari wants to talk with her about her future, but she resists. She'll stick with Nick. Ari refrains from saying she's making a mistake.

It's eighteen months later. Ari is waiting to board his plane — he's flying to a conference in Denver — waiting to board when, looking across the center aisle toward another gate, he sees Nick Shorr. Ari turns away, but Nick has spotted him and waves.

He's looking good, Nick, not like someone who's been in prison. He's oddly well dressed for a plane. Most passengers — including Ari himself — wear sweat shirts, jeans or chinos, winter parkas. Nick has dressed in a business suit, off-white shirt, silk tie; over his arm he carries a London Fog trench coat. Ari snaps a mental picture to tell Lori. He turns away to avoid being seen.

"Ari!" Nick calls. "Ari!"

No way to ignore him. They meet in the aisle between the two gates. "How are you, Rabbi?"

Ari touches his chest. "As you see me. As you see me. Well. It seems you've landed on your feet."

"Oh, yes. You could definitely say that. I'm working for a business based in Boston. A non-profit. Nancy's in the ladies' room. We're taking a little vacation. Remember, Ari, when we all went to St. Johns? How's your wife?"

Ari doesn't answer. He could say that he's never gotten over what Nick did — that a month ago he decided to accept the offer to be rabbi, beginning in the summer, of a larger synagogue in the Boston suburbs. But he won't give Nick the satisfaction.

"B'nai Shalom has gotten much of the money back," Ari says. "Did you know that? It seems we were insured against theft. Including embezzlement."

"I know. I did that for you—bought it for you just in case." Nick laughs, laughs, the sound drowned out by the announcement: Nick's plane is ready for boarding first-class passengers and Platinum card holders. Here comes Nancy. Spotting Ari she turns away.

"I think we're supposed to board, Nick," she says and walks off, rolling a small carry-on behind her.

"*You* bought us the theft insurance?"

Nick smiles benevolently. "It's the least I could do, Rabbi—in case my little . . . bonuses were discovered." He beams, taps Ari on the shoulder, and, following Nancy to the gate, waving his fingers high in the air to say goodbye, calls back, "Of course the insurance people insisted I pay them back, but we negotiated excellent terms."

"So . . . who do you work for now?" Ari calls after him. "Who'd you say you work for now?" But Nick follows Nancy to the door. Stopping before the agent checking his boarding pass, he turns, and, as if Ari were an audience, gives him a final grin, spreads his arms wide, kisses his fingers, then rolls his suitcase through the door and down the ramp.

The electronic sign over the door:

Flight 3405 . . . Cancun.

Once there was a man who trusted and trusted. An open-hearted man who counted on everyone's good faith. And now? Now he's growing up. Is that a good thing? Lori thinks so. But it's a little sad. If he hasn't put up

between him and the world a wall of suspicion, he has at
least put up a locked gate. He comes out to do good work.
But the key — oh, the key he puts in his pocket and doesn't
give out to many people.

* * *

Forgiveness

AT EVERY SYNAGOGUE the month of Elul at the end of summer is exhausting for the leadership of the congregation and for the rabbi — as it is at B'nai Shalom (Children of Peace), in Brookline, Massachusetts. The Ritual Committee has to organize services and distribute honors: This one will come up to the bima to bless the Torah, that one will carry the Torah scroll through the aisles. Services at Rosh Hashanah and Yom Kippur are for many Jews the only services they attend all year.

The long wall of the small sanctuary at B'nai Shalom accordions away, making the large sanctuary larger. Rabbi Ari will play to a packed house. So he's busy preparing sermons, talking to the cantor, and practicing the *nusach* (the melody) traditional for the High Holidays.

Sam Schulman, who leads a morning service most Tuesdays, feels for Ari — Rabbi Ari Stein — Ari's in an especially tough position this year. At the start of summer the board treasurer discovered that, over a period of five years, almost a quarter of a million dollars had been embezzled from B'nai Shalom. The Executive Director agreed to plead guilty in exchange for serving minimal time in prison. Some money he paid back, some was paid by insurance. Some is gone forever. Sam knows that Ari will have to speak about the loss while not making too much of it—he has to keep the community together.

Elul, the month surrounding High Holidays, is a time of spiritual preparation. We are to change our lives. On Rosh Hashanah, the New Year—we are inscribed in the Book of Life; ten days later, Yom Kippur, as we pray for change in ourselves and for forgiveness, we are judged, the Book sealed. We live, we die; we prosper, we fail to prosper. God has judged.

Who believes this literally? Maybe only the Orthodox. Yet as myth, communal shaping of our lives, it has great power. It's not theoretical; it enters our hearts. Surely it has power over Sam Schulman. Neither believing nor disbelieving, he lives as if the holy power of the Days of Awe rumbled through him. Shaken by the blast of the shofar—a curving trumpet made of a ram's horn—we are enjoined to listen, and maybe tremble. Sam lives, we live, much of Rosh Hashanah and Yom Kippur, *as if* the Holy One watched over and judged us all.

The rest of the time Sam teaches Nineteenth Century Novel at Boston University.

The shofar blast is heard not only on Rosh Hashanah and at the very end of Yom Kippur services, but also at weekday services the month of Elul, just before High Holidays. Tuesday mornings throughout the year at B'nai Shalom a minyan meets. Ten or more if they're lucky.

During Elul, two or three members of the minyan bring their shofars and blow them together. The air quivers in a prescribed pattern of blasts—long, short, very short, finally very long—sounds meant to raze your ordinary consciousness and blast you into *Teshuvah*—repentance, a turning to God.

This is a story about Teshuvah.

On a Tuesday morning at the beginning of Elul, Sam is happy to see Deborah Pearl come into the small sanctuary. Her first time. She sits next to Kate, Sam's fiancée. It's hard to bring together at 7:30 in the morning ten adult Jews—a complete minyan—allowing them to pray as a community—to say the Barechu and Kaddish. Counting in his head, he thinks now that Deborah's come, they'll make it today. Sam knows Deborah's recent story the way most inner members of the synagogue know it: her husband Dave left her for a young colleague. Sam sighs. He feels for her. Deborah is, fortunately, a free-lance writer; she's able to adjust her time and as a single parent take care of her eight-year-old daughter.

At the end of the service, the blast of the shofar—blown, this morning, by a professor of physics from M.I.T.—echoes through the small sanctuary.

The next Tuesday morning Sam is surprised: Deborah's back. She listens, eyes closed, to the harsh blare of the shofar. After that service, just about everyone gone, she sits watching Sam take off tefillin and fold away tallis.

"I wonder," she says. "Do you have a minute, Sam?

I'd like to speak with you. It's about Teshuvah. Do you remember, I was in that adult education class you led?"

God, does he ever! She talked and talked. Feverishly. It rankled him — others didn't get to speak. She was articulate, but she seemed more interested in herself-saying than in *what* she was saying. He was fooled at first — hard for him not to give the benefit of the doubt to a clever, pretty woman, with wild black hair, in long dresses that reveal her figure. But he stopped calling on her so often — wouldn't let her take over. Still, he tried to remain patient. Beneath all that talk, he told himself, there's true longing.

"I don't want to talk to the Rabbi," she says. "I guess I'd be frightened. But I thought *you* might be a big help — about guilt and, you know, repentance. Maybe point me in the Right Direction. You probably don't remember, but in that class we spoke about Yom Kippur and forgiveness. Yom Kippur is meant to wipe clean a sin against God. But, according to the Talmud" — Deborah takes a folded slip of paper from her purse and reads from a printout — "*For sins committed against other human beings, Yom Kippur does not atone. Prayer is not sufficient. We have to beg forgiveness from those against whom we've sinned.*"

"That's right. Many sources tell us that. So, Deborah, do you need to forgive someone? Or ask someone for forgiveness?"

They sit in adjoining chairs, and she takes a deep breath and tells Sam her story.

Amelia Ross has been Deborah's closest friend. "You know Amelia?"

"I know who she is. I was on a committee with her."

Well, when Deborah was slogging through her separation and divorce, Amelia held her hand. Literally Held Her Hand. This was two summers ago. Some days after work, they'd sit on a bench at the Esplanade by the Charles and Amelia would take Deborah's hand.

" 'They're going to think we're lovers,' I whispered. I mean, like, holding my *hand*?"

" 'I don't care,' Amelia said, and she patted my hand. 'Do you really care?' "

"And I didn't. She soothed me."

And once or twice a week Deborah and her daughter Susan went to Amelia and Rob's for dinner. The women were proud of being able to share cooking fluidly, dancing around each other preparing food while Susan practiced piano or hung out with Amelia's son, Noah. When Rob, who worked hard as a lawyer, a specialist in mergers and acquisitions, came home, dragged out, all was ready. He poured drinks.

The two couples met in birthing class eight years before. They had babies at the same time, joined B'nai Shalom at the same time. When one of the women took on a project at the synagogue—organizing the auction, laying out food for a scholar's talk—the other joined in. The men were good casual friends. Now, Deborah's ex, Dave, has moved to California to take a new position and begin a new family with a woman colleague — "twenty years younger," she tells Sam, "can you imagine?" — and Deborah and her daughter ate often at her friends' apartment.

"One night Rob laughed, 'My God. The adults in this here dining room, we're practically a *ménage a trois.'*

"Then, embarrassed, he changed it: 'I mean, like . . . a commune. We share meals.'

"So, Sam, I told them 'I *don't* mean to take advantage. Susan and I are probably here too often. You two have been such a comfort.' Which is true!

"But Rob said, 'Please! Not at all. *Please.'* And I couldn't help wondering, Sam: Did he really *mean* a *ménage a trois?* And I couldn't meet Rob's eyes. I must have turned forty-seven shades of red."

Often, Deborah says Rob drove her and Susan home the few blocks to her apartment. He drove that night — night of the "*ménage à trois.*" "And Rob told me, 'What I said before, you really misunderstood. I was celebrating, not complaining.'

"And while we were waiting for the light to change, he whispered so Susan wouldn't hear, 'You, you're the spark in my eyes, Deborah.'"

He didn't look at her; he had looked straight ahead, both hands holding the wheel.

Sam listens. Deborah goes on and on, as she went on and on in class. But he can see she's in pain. He lets her tell about her feelings:

Her feelings when Rob said she was the spark in his eyes.

Her feelings about her beloved friend.

Her feelings about Rob, her beloved friend's attractive husband.

And now (Deborah tells Sam), a new narrative begins to write itself. "You see where this is going, Sam?"

He nods, nods, puts a hand to his chest, sighs. He's trying to remain non-judgmental. *Judge everyone on the side of merit.* So says the Talmud. But Deborah, oh, she's such a child! Her feelings, her feelings. It's all about her. Still, he thinks, a child can suffer. Deborah's really suffering. He remembers how aggravated he became when Rabbi Ari spoke about Nick, the embezzling bastard, as 'Poor man.' Ari felt that anyone who could betray friends and a community that's based on the love of justice, must be, *even if he didn't know it*, deeply suffering. That's how Sam feels about this woman, who's about to tell him how she betrayed her best friend: *Poor woman.*

What was happening, God knows (and Deborah affirms) she hadn't planned. Course not. In the dark car, feelings spilled from her. The times she and Rob had been together, maybe these feelings were always there, unrecognized. "You think so, Sam? I mean, haven't I always kept them tucked away in a pocket of consciousness?"

"And now you're feeling guilty?" He says this by rote; Sam would prefer to be alone over a cup of coffee at Starbuck's.

"No, no. Wait. I haven't told you the half . . . . Sam? You have a few more minutes?"

He looks at his watch. "Faculty Personnel Committee isn't until eleven. Sure. Go on."

"A little flirtation, well, that's one thing," Deborah says. "But I certainly didn't intend to betray my friend. You think I was fooling myself, Sam?"

"I'm really not a therapist, Deborah. And I'm not a priest."

Still, Deborah goes on, hadn't she listened to Amelia complain about her marriage, about how busy Rob is, how indifferent Rob seems? Amelia is principal of a private school, K through six, and most of the time she doesn't talk about her marriage—she tells Deborah how excited she is with changes she's brought to the school. "Amelia isn't a complainer. Me, I'm sometimes a complainer," Deborah says. "I know it. Not Amelia. But sometimes Amelia spills out teeny grumbles about Rob. I think what happened, Sam, is I reshaped the story Amelia was telling me. Like: *Rob has for a long time been dissatisfied with Amelia. Rob has for a long time been in love with me.* Of course that doesn't mean I intended to *do* anything about it."

But one night the three of them and the two kids stay up a little late at Rob's and Amelia's, and when Rob drives Deborah home, Susan falls asleep in the car, so Rob carries Suze upstairs and puts her to bed. And there they are in the dark living room, Rob and Deborah, and they take each other's hands and stand breathing, breathing, breathing. They just look at each other. That's absolutely all, so ludicrous, the two of them like teenagers. Rob's got this wonderful smile. Then Deborah walks him to the door and as always, they kiss, kiss like friends. Deborah can't sleep half the night. She keeps rewriting and rewriting the scene. What she should have said. What she should have done.

"Then the next day Rob calls And he tells me what, I guess, I've been wanting to hear. 'You know this is inevitable,' he says. 'Don't you?'

"Oh, *God*, Sam."

Silence in the small sanctuary now, a long silence on the phone that day. Deborah imitates Rob's powerful baritone: "Can we get together for lunch tomorrow?"

"So I said, 'We'll talk. We should talk. I'll make you lunch.'"

"When was all this?" Sam asks.

"Oh . . . six months, seven months ago."

And so they meet at her apartment, and Susan is of course at school, and, she says to Sam, what did she *think* was going to happen? But omigod, it's as if she were watching events beyond her control. "You know — like on a roller coaster."

He wants to ask: Was inviting the man for lunch at your house also uncontrollable? You couldn't find a restaurant in Boston? He doesn't ask.

We're not bound to do a single thing, she says to herself

as she prepares the *salade nicoise*. But she *does* feel bound —
her hands are tied, what can she do? — and to protect her
she secrets away the idea that being bound diminishes her
betrayal. *If* we step over the line. *Not* that it's inevitable.
No. We can simply stay friends.

"Oh, sure," she says now. "Sure."

Now she's in tears, tears running down her face, and
Sam doesn't know what's best to do. Tell her she's fooling
herself? Suggest she see a therapist? He doesn't. He just
listens. Through tears she talks.

"Rob's a big, hairy man," she tells Sam — "hair on his
chest, hair on his back — a thick muscled man who works
out in the gym. You don't mind if I speak like this? I
shouldn't. I know I shouldn't. Stop me if you want, Sam."

She knows Rob's body from swims on St. John's when
the two families vacationed together. It's very exciting to
touch him, to transgress; let's admit it, the transgression
itself is terribly exciting. Just to touch him through a business shirt, then to undo his tie and — you know, like — open
the buttons of his shirt, both of us laughing like children.
You know Rob's beautiful little laugh? And then be silent
with each other. *You* know.

She's sure she isn't as beautiful as Amelia. "God!
Amelia is lean like a girl, small, a dancer, a runner. Me,
I'm soft, my hair wild and black, not like Amelia's neat
page-boy blonde."

Sam figures she wants him to tell her she's beautiful.
He refrains.

"In my mind Amelia was in the bedroom with Rob and me. A *ménage a trois* for real."

She leads Rob to the bed where she and Dave, her ex, have made love so often in their ten years together. It's raining out, a slant rain against the windows. Somehow that matters. She thinks that if it had been sunny out, she would likely have turned him away, but that in the gray rainy day she couldn't hold back from him. "You understand, Sam?"

They drop their clothes on the floor, and part of the delight is in so totally replacing Dave. "As if it meant I hadn't lost anything. It was both brand new and so completely *home*."

"And now," he says, wanting to wrap this up and get to his office, "you're feeling guilty?"

She's a little hurt by his summation. "There's much more, Sam."

He makes gestures of apology for interrupting.

Deborah plays with her scarf. "After that we were careful. We didn't get together a lot. Rob said, 'We don't want to turn our lives into chaos, do we? And no, no, we certainly did not. The very last thing we wanted. I said to Rob, 'It's a heavy responsibility to be mature enough not to let love run away with us.'"

"But Amelia found out?"

"Not exactly. Well, yes, but not *yet*. The next thing is, Amelia was diagnosed with cancer, pancreatic cancer. Which is weird, because Amelia is a runner; she doesn't smoke, she eats a diet rich in fruits and vegetables. She doesn't look sick at first. She loses weight and is kind of pleased with herself, though she's never been fat. She said, 'I'm back to my weight just after college, I have to take in all my clothes. A nice problem, if you ask me.' But sometimes, she got really sad and I hated myself. I shopped for her, I bought new clothes for her."

Then one day Amelia calls Deborah. They meet at the Esplanade by the Charles, and Amelia takes Deborah's hand as if it were Deborah who needed comforting. Amelia soothes. "And she tells me, 'It's still bearable. All I want is not to have a lot of pain. I'm a coward when it comes to pain. And I want to know that Noah will be okay. And Rob.'

"So I said, 'You know how much they'll miss you.' And here's the thing, Sam. Amelia looks into my eyes and says, 'You'll help, I know you will. You'll help.'

"I knew what she was suggesting. If she dies, *when* she dies, I might take her place, might make a new family — with Susan and Noah and Rob. God! If Rob and I had only waited! It would be so different."

Too late now. Without a word spoken, Rob and Deborah stop seeing each other. And the more they stay away from each other the more desperately in love Deborah feels — and the more guilty. "Already Amelia is practically gone, and in my head I've taken her place, and the children are like brother and sister, and we both, Rob and Deborah, remember Amelia with love, so much love."

It doesn't happen that way.

Now they talk on the phone, Deborah and Amelia, nearly every day. And Deborah asks and asks, how is the pain, how is your appetite? And Amelia tells her how loving Rob has become—though, she says, he's always been loving. But there are none of the little quarrels now. Deborah wants to find out, Have you been, you know, *close* to Rob? She can't bring herself to ask.

"I see why you're thinking of Yom Kippur," Sam says, feeling the moral gravity of what the three of them are going through. "How do you atone?"

"Yes. But there's more."

Sam sits back and stops fighting it. He surrenders his morning.

With Amelia sick, Deborah often makes dinner for the family, separate food for Amelia. Afternoons, she visits Amelia, gives her massages, feels how flaccid her muscle tone is becoming, how the ribs and collar bone are showing.

She never speaks to Rob now. Rob never calls her. When they're together, the three of them, they avoid each other. But one night, late, depressed, Deborah calls. She asks, Is Amelia awake? No, he says, no, she's been asleep for hours. So Deborah tells him how she loves him, and she tells him how hard this playacting is.

"I said, like, 'How are we going to handle the guilt? I feel so awful about you and me. What's especially terrible, it's that I find myself longing for an ending, waiting for her to leave us.'

"And Amelia *wasn't* asleep. No. Half asleep, she picked up the phone in the bedroom and was awake and couldn't stop listening in."

"Oh! How awful — awful for Amelia," Sam says. "Oh!"

"Yes! Awful! And for *me*! Imagine! Awful. When I called the next morning, she said, like, 'I'm not feeling well enough to see you.'"

Deborah takes that at face value. As she imagines it, Amelia is coming close to the end. Hanging up the phone, Deborah cries, suffering, miserable that she'll lose her friend, her best friend — and miserable that, partly, partly, she *wants* to lose her.

Then a phone call from Rob. Can we meet?

Late summer. A bench in the Boston Gardens. Rob is there first. He stands up and kisses her, the kiss of a friend. At once she grows uneasy. "'How's Amelia?'

"He says, 'Deborah, she *heard*, she picked up the phone when you called.'

"'Oh, my God.' That's all I could say."

Now she says it over and over, "Oh, my God, oh, my God," the pain building each time she says the words, each time she remembers what she said on the phone. Nothing can make it right, nothing she can do. "So I said, 'Rob? What'd you tell her?'

"And he says, 'What could I say? Could I say anything?'

"I said to him, 'It was mostly my guilt talking. Not being able to stand it. A person has all kinds of feelings.

Sure I wanted this to end. I also love her. I love Amelia very much.'

"'I guess it's too late for love,' Rob says. 'Amelia hates you.'

"Which isn't fair," Deborah says to Sam. "I could feel his coldness. It's all over. Unfair! As if it was all me, only me, *my* sin. What about Rob? Why should he lay it all on me? And then Rob said, 'Oh. Yes. I forgot. I did say something to her. I told her we'd imagined she'd want us to be together.' Then he added, 'That didn't go over so well, Deb.'"

Now Sam and Deborah sit, both of them considering the ending of this love of hers, this guilt, especially the guilt. "What should I do, Sam?"

"What do you think? Really. You tell me. What do you think? When you asked me to listen, you knew. Didn't you know?"

"You're going to tell me, go on my knees, beg her forgiveness, right? Omigod. She'll slap my face."

"Maybe she will. Deborah, I'm not telling you what to do. But if you're asking what would the tradition tell you? If you're asking what's the way to seek atonement? According to Jewish tradition, you said it yourself: Prayer isn't enough. Inner repentance isn't sufficient."

"Right, oh, right. Well, thank you, Sam, for listening to me blabber on."

"Is she dying? Amelia?"

"She may not last another month. Sam? Actually,

actually . . . I love her. I do. I love her — I mean when we're talking just *love*, you know? — more than I love Rob. She's my shining star. The spark in *my* eyes. No. My compass."

* * *

Yom Kippur services in B'nai Shalom — the large, even grandiose sanctuary of marble and stained glass. The wall of the small sanctuary has been folded back. Sam sits with Gabriel, his son, and with Kate. He knows Gabriel won't stay for the Musaf service. He'll leave at Yiskor, the service remembering the dead. Sam is happy that he attends at all. Kate, soon to marry Sam, will stay beside him.

Everyone has begun a fast that started yesterday at sunset. By the time we break our fast, twenty-five hours after we begin, we're weak, maybe lightheaded. It helps bring us into a different consciousness.

Sam sees Deborah a few rows away across the room. Behind her and to the side, at the end of a row, Amelia and Rob. Looking around, she spots Sam and quickly looks away. Is she afraid that his presence will feel like judgment? — that he'll press her to speak to Amelia, morally force her to speak?

Rabbi Ari, young, early forties, charismatic, writer of two books and a weekly column in a Jewish online paper, offers words of Torah this morning. The Torah scroll has been bound, the chazzan sits down and the Rabbi speaks about repentance and forgiveness at Yom Kippur.

"We were all victims of a thief. We all suffered damage from the embezzlement. Should the thief, whom we all trusted and liked, go up to each of you and confess? And if he did, would you forgive? Repentance and forgiveness is a vehicle of growth for the one repenting and for the one forgiving."

"Maybe," Ari says, "you've hurt someone who's in this very room, in this community, maybe the person sitting right next to you. Maybe somewhere in this old sanctuary there's a person you've insulted—or maybe you're holding a grudge and you'd like to let it go—to forgive. Are you thinking of speaking to that person? Maybe you can't do it right now, but you can do it later . . . ."

He pauses.

"You might want to close your eyes and think about this."

The shofar won't be blown until the end of the final service today—when the final prayers are chanted and the Gates of Mercy close. Before they close we will make a final pitch to God, chant over and over. We beg, we demand. Then many hold up their shofarim and blast in cacophonous concert. Rabbi Ari is a strong shofar blower; he has a twisting, four-foot ram's horn, hollowed to make a chamber for sound that can blast open ordinary consciousness. From all parts of the sanctuary shofarim— three, four, maybe ten!—will blare, as lights dim and our souls are, if they ever are, awake.

But that's not until this evening.

This morning, as we prepare to open our souls, Sam's eye is on Deborah, halfway across the room. He imagines — can't really see but imagines — heat filling Deborah's face. He hasn't told Rabbi Ari her story, but the Rabbi's talk, it seems as if it were directed to her. She may be wondering if he, Sam, has said something.

Three rows behind her are Amelia and Rob. Deborah is on the aisle. All she has to do is stand up and go to Amelia. So simple. Out of the corner of his eye he keeps watching. *Go!* He whispers to himself, Go on, go up to Amelia. Maybe not to say anything, just to lean past Rob and hug Amelia.

Would Amelia permit Deborah to come close? Or would she turn away?

Deborah looks around, seems about to stand, she's going to do it!

No! She can't do it. Her betrayal of Amelia is breaking her heart, Sam knows; it breaks her heart to think Amelia will die without a reconciliation. And look at Amelia: so thin, so weak, her hair too glossy — a wig.

Deborah sits eyes closed.

Now Sam finds tears blurring his own eyes — because, look! — it's Amelia who has the strength to come over. She stands up, a little shaky, with the help of a cane she walks very slowly down the aisle, her hand on the pew backs. As if *she* were the one who needed to ask forgiveness!

Sam sees: Deborah makes room. Deborah makes room for Amelia on the hard bench. They're touching hip to hip. They look at each other and he's sure that, all the while, Deborah must be talking, saying, I'm so sorry, I'm so sorry, I love you, I'm so sorry. And Amelia runs her fingers over Deborah's cheeks and must be saying, I forgive you, I forgive you everything. Forgive me. I so hated you.

Sam looks at Rob. Rob Cole is ignoring or pretending to ignore Amelia and Deborah. Big shoulders hunched under the blue and white tallis, maybe he's watching the two women out of the corner of his eye.

We're about to begin *Yiskor*, the remembrance of our beloved dead. Sam will remember his parents, he'll remember his beloved Bennie, who died of cancer as a third year student at Yale. Most of the congregants are whispering to one another or reading in the prayer book for High Holidays, waiting for the Rabbi to begin. One or two seem to notice the two women weeping, but after all, this is Yom Kippur—service of personal and communal repentance. All sorts of passions are felt.

He sees that Deborah and Amelia hang on one another and weep. Amelia's the one comforting. Oh! Deborah's repentance is the repentance of a child; Amelia's is deep, real.

Deborah is too far from Sam to speak. And he's not, after all, what's important. Still, she does turn to look at him and she nods. Wants him to know. *See?*

It's very good. He himself is almost crying. Amelia's gesture: how beautiful!

The chazzan is chanting, and soon Yiskor—*May God remember* . . . the service recalling our beloved ones gone from us, will begin, and Sam will remember his mother, his father, his son Bennie. And he foresees that next year they'll be remembering Amelia. Deborah hugs Amelia closer, as if she's already mourning, as if she already lost her friend. Clearly, they don't care who watches them. They're in a pool of being that separates them from everyone, as if they were surrounded by a shimmer of light.

* * *